THE STRANGE MESSAGE
IN THE PARCHMENT

A SHEEP farmer receives a mysterious telephone call shortly after he buys a series of pictures painted on parchment. "Decipher the message in the parchment and right a great wrong," the voice says. Puzzled, the owner asks Nancy to help.

With Junie, his daughter, Nancy tracks down a kidnapper and a group of extortionists. Clues weave in and out of several puzzles, two of which are linked with Italy. Is there a connection between the message in the parchment and a boy artist on another farm? And who is responsible for the atmosphere of fear in the neighborhood?

After several harrowing experiences, Nancy begins to tighten the net around a ruthless villain and calls on the assistance of her friends Ned, Burt, Dave, Bess and George to bring his nefarious schemes to a dead end.

The ram got ready to toss Nancy into the air.

The Strange Message in the Parchment

BY CAROLYN KEENE

GROSSET & DUNLAP
Publishers • New York
A member of The Putnam & Grosset Group

PRINTED ON RECYCLED PAPER

Contents

The Strange Message in the Parchment

CHAPTER I

Stolen!

"IT's perfectly beautiful!" Nancy exclaimed.

She was standing in front of a long mirror in the Drew hallway, admiring herself in a sheepskin jacket. Near her stood a girl of the same age, eighteen. The two were of identical height and slender, but Nancy was a strawberry blond with blue eyes, while the other girl had brown hair and eyes.

"Junie Flockhart, you're a darling!" Nancy said, hugging her friend, a former schoolmate. Junie's family had moved many miles away, to a large sheep farm.

Junie smiled. "You know, Nancy, you were always one of my father's favorites. When I told him I was coming here to visit, he sent you this gift. By the way, how would you like to solve a mystery for him?"

Nancy's eyes sparkled. A mystery!

At this moment a motherly, middle-aged woman came into the hallway to greet Junie and admire the sheepskin jacket. She was Hannah Gruen, the Drews' housekeeper, who had been a mother to Nancy since the girl was three and her own mother had passed away.

"Did your father make the jacket?" Hannah asked Junie.

"Yes," she replied. "At one end of Triple Creek Farm he has a factory that produces sheepskin articles. Dad also makes parchment from the sheep's skins.

"He has a marvelous collection of parchments from all over the world," Junie went on. "Some are very old. A few have illuminated writing on them in foreign languages; others have beautiful painted pictures."

"I'd love to see them," Nancy put in.

"You will if you come home with me to solve the mystery. My father has a parchment that has four lovely small paintings on it. He is intrigued by the parchment because of a strange phone call he received soon after he bought it. A man who didn't give his name said the picture had a message. Anyone who could figure it out would bring happiness and comfort to several people, and right an old wrong."

"That's strange," Nancy replied. "If the man knew this, why didn't he tell the whole story?"

"He hung up abruptly," Junie answered, "as

if someone had approached him and he couldn't say any more. Everyone in our family has tried and failed to decipher the meaning of the picture."

"I'd like to try to solve the mystery," Nancy said. "When do I start?"

"As soon as you can get ready. And say, why don't we have a house party? Ned, Burt, Dave, Bess, George, and my date, Dan. I know you'll like him."

"That's a wonderful idea," Nancy replied. "What do you think, Hannah?"

Mrs. Gruen smiled. "The instant I heard there was a mystery to solve at Triple Creek Farm, I knew you'd want to go. I think the idea is great. If your father hasn't any special work for his sleuthing daughter, I'm sure he'll agree."

Nancy took off the sheepskin jacket and laid it on a chair in the living room for her father to see when he came home. Then she went upstairs with Hannah and Junie to look through her closet and select appropriate clothing for the trip.

"Don't bother with a lot of dresses," Junie said. "At the farm we just about live in jeans, shirts, and jackets."

All this time Hannah Gruen had been grinning. "Junie, you've never seen Nancy when she's trying to solve a mystery. She's like a hound on a scent and never gives up until she has caught the villain!"

Junie was about to say something, but just then Nancy whispered, "Listen! I heard the front door close softly. Let's find out who's there."

She and Junie hurried down the stairs. No one was in sight and when Nancy called out, asking who was in the house, there was no answer. Then she noticed something strange.

"My new jacket is gone!" Nancy cried.

The girls stared at the empty chair.

"My beautiful sheepskin jacket must have been stolen!" Nancy exclaimed.

She rushed to the front door and opened it wide, just in time to see a girl disappearing around the end of the curved driveway. She was wearing the sheepskin jacket!

"Let's chase her!" Nancy urged. She whistled for her little terrier, Togo, who hurried from the kitchen. "Come on, old boy! We must catch a thief."

Togo followed her and Junie out the door. For a few seconds the dog ran alongside Nancy. As soon as they reached the street, however, and his mistress pointed to the fleeing thief, he knew what he was supposed to do and bounded off. The stranger had a good head start and was running like a trained athlete.

"We'll never catch her," Junie said.

"She must be a professional thief," Nancy added. "She was so quiet she didn't even disturb Togo."

"Come on, Togo! We must catch a thief!"

Junie wondered how the girl had known about the coat. "Of course I carried it in a plastic see-through bag," she said. "That girl may have noticed it and followed me from the train to your house."

Nancy nodded. "She may have been spying and when we went upstairs, she came in. But how did she get in?"

By now Togo had almost caught up to the stranger. At the same moment all three girls saw a policeman in the distance. The thief, realizing it was useless to proceed, quickly turned into a driveway.

By the time Nancy and Junie reached the spot, the suspect was out of sight. Togo was returning, however, to present them with a chunk of cloth, which he held in his teeth. Nancy reached down and took it.

"This is a piece from that sneak thief's skirt!" she exclaimed. "What a great clue! Togo, you're a clever little dog."

Togo barked as though he were urging Nancy to continue the search. "Maybe the thief is hiding," Nancy said.

The girls raced down the driveway to the rear of the property, where there was a hedge. Nancy's jacket lay on the ground in front of it! Togo pulled it along the ground, growling all the time.

Nancy picked it up. "Togo, you're marvelous!

You scared that girl into discarding the jacket when you took a piece out of her skirt!"

"Let's go on!" Junie urged. "Maybe we can catch her."

The girls parted the hedge and went through. The thief was not in sight. Trying to guess which direction she had taken, they ran into the adjoining yard. Here the two searchers separated, one going along the left side of the house, the other to the right.

Within a few seconds they met on the front sidewalk and looked up and down the street. There was no sign of the person they wanted.

Nancy heaved a sigh. "Anyway," she said, "I'm thankful to have my beautiful jacket back. And Togo got a good clue we can take to the police."

The little dog was jumping and barking. Junie looked puzzled.

"Togo is asking for further instructions from me," Nancy explained. She leaned over and patted him once more. "He's eager to continue the case. I—"

Nancy stopped speaking abruptly when Togo barked again. This time he leaped to the pavement and ran alongside a car that was speeding down the street.

"What's Togo doing that for?" Junie asked.

Without replying, Nancy started running also. Her first thought was to keep Togo from being killed if the driver, either accidentally or deliberately, swerved and hit him.

"Togo, come back!" she cried out.

The little dog paid no attention. Suddenly Nancy caught a glimpse of the young woman on the passenger side and realized why. The dress matched the sample Togo had snatched from the thief's skirt!

The car's driver, evidently sensing the situation, put on speed. Out of breath, Nancy stopped. She was in time to catch the number on the license plate and memorize it. Togo had given up the chase, too, and returned to Nancy on the sidewalk.

"Thank you, Togo," she said, hugging him. "Now we'll go."

Junie hurried up to them and was told of Nancy's discovery. She was astounded at the rapidity with which clues were mounting.

"All you have to do," she said, "is report the license number to the police. They'll learn who the car's owner is, the name of his passenger, and catch the thief."

"I hope it will be that easy," Nancy said. "But—"

"But what?" Junie asked.

"The driver may not be the owner of the car."

"You mean, he might have stolen it?"

"Right. If he did, he'll probably abandon it. Another possibility is that the driver does not know his passenger. She could have hitchhiked and not given her name."

Junie's look of hope faded. "And here I thought it would be easy. Well, it may still be. Let's think positive, Nancy, and go to the police with a report."

CHAPTER II

Triple Creek Farm

"LET's go back to the house first and get my car," Nancy suggested. "It's some distance to the police station. Then we'll show Chief McGinnis the shred from the thief's dress and the jacket. He's a good friend of mine."

Junie asked, "What can the police find out from the jacket?"

"Sometimes they discover the most amazing facts about the person who wore a garment."

"Like what?"

"Oh, the blood type, kind of skin, height, weight, male or female—"

By this time her friend from Triple Creek Farm was laughing. "Don't tell me any more. I'm lost already."

When they reached the house, Nancy took Togo inside and told Hannah where they were going. Then, taking along the new jacket, Nancy backed her sleek blue car out of the garage and drove to headquarters. Chief McGinnis greeted the girls enthusiastically.

"Nancy, I know you have come to tell me about a mystery. I see it in your eyes. What is it this time?"

Nancy grinned, then introduced Junie. She told the middle-aged, good-natured man she was trying to track down a thief.

"Junie brought me this beautiful jacket from her father's sheep farm, but a short while later, a girl sneaked into our house and stole it."

Chief McGinnis looked puzzled. "You say *this* jacket was stolen?"

"It was. But we got it back." Nancy told him about the whole incident and produced the piece of material from the thief's skirt. Her eyes twinkled. "You see, Chief McGinnis, I even have Togo trained to be a detective."

"He's very clever. Maybe you ought to put him into our Canine Corps!" the chief replied. Then he promised to alert his men and have them track down the thief, using the shred of cloth she had brought as a clue. Nancy told him the license number of the car in which the girl had escaped.

"I'll trace it at once," Chief McGinnis said.

Nancy explained that the thief had actually worn the coat and run in it for several blocks. "Then she saw a policeman ahead, and Togo was close to her heels. So she threw the jacket onto a hedge. Do you think you might find any clues to her from this?"

"I don't know. But if you'll leave it here, together with the cloth, I'll have our lab inspect them carefully."

Nancy thanked the officer and the two girls said good-by. That evening Mr. Drew was amazed to hear the story, and wondered how the thief had entered their home. Nobody could explain it and for several seconds there was silence in the living room, where the family had gathered with their guest.

Suddenly Togo, who had been lying on the floor with his ears cocked, jumped up, stood on his hind legs, and walked around.

Junie laughed. "How cute!" she remarked. "Not only is he a detective dog, but a trick dog!"

Nancy explained that there was more to the gesture than that. Whenever Togo was trying to convey a message to anyone in the family, he would do this. The little dog now dropped to all fours and hurried to the front door. Nancy followed and asked the others to join her.

As they watched, Togo got up again on his hind legs and held the handle of the door in his forepaws. Next he put his teeth around the handle and presto! the door opened. The Drews and Junie looked at the animal in astonishment.

"You little scamp!" Nancy said to him. "You're

the one that left the door open so the thief could come in!"

Togo acted very pleased with himself. He danced around some more and gave several short barks.

"That was a neat trick," Mr. Drew remarked, "but I think we'll have to put an extra lock on the door. One that Togo can't reach and open for burglars."

Togo seemed to understand. His tail dropped, a sad look came to his eyes, and he lay down.

As Nancy patted him, she told her father about the invitation to Triple Creek Farm. "Bess and George and also Ned, Dave, and Burt are to be invited for a house party up there."

The lawyer's eyes twinkled. "With a mystery to solve and a house party included, I don't see how you could refuse."

Nancy kissed her father, then immediately went to call her friends and give them the exciting invitation. Nancy would go ahead with Junie; the other guests were to follow later.

While she was on the phone, Mr. Drew said to Junie with boyish pride, "I have a few sheepskins of my own. Come with me and I'll show them to you."

He led her into his study. Between bookcases and pictures hung framed diplomas. One was from high school, another from college, and the third and most impressive was from law school.

"I see you graduated from all three places with honors," Junie said. "My congratulations!"

"Thank you," the lawyer replied. "The other day we were discussing the laws governing the ownership of sheep in your state. If you have a flock and any of the sheep are killed by wild animals, will the state reimburse the owner for his loss?"

"Yes," Junie replied. "And wild dogs are also classed under the heading of wild animals. It has always amazed me how dogs differ. Wild dogs will kill sheep and eat them, but those that have been reared from puppies by human beings love the sheep. They guard them and take care of them. We have several sheep dogs at the farm. My favorite is Rover."

The conversation was interrupted by Nancy, who reported that all of their friends would be able to visit Triple Creek Farm.

"Bess and George can make it next weekend," she said, "but the boys are uncertain when they can come. They'll try to visit at the same time as the girls."

Nancy went on to say that her friend Ned Nickerson had told her about an interesting artist who lived in the vicinity of Triple Creek Farm. She asked Junie if she had ever heard of Vincenzo Caspari.

Junie shook her head. "I never have, but my parents may know him. Why did Ned mention him?"

"I was telling Ned about the strange phone call regarding the parchment. He said this man might be able to help us."

The girls went to bed early and were up at seven o'clock, packing their bags. By nine they drove off, with good wishes from Mr. Drew and Hannah Gruen. They took turns driving Nancy's car, since it was a long ride. Afternoon shadows were lengthening as the travelers finally reached the six-hundred acre Triple Creek Farm.

"What a wonderful place!" Nancy exclaimed, as Junie turned into a long lane that led to the farmhouse.

Though the building had many wings and extensions in every direction, it was attractive and inviting. Mr. and Mrs. Flockhart were there to welcome the girls.

The owner was a large, handsome man with graying hair. Nancy thought his beautiful gray eyes looked as if they had stars shining in them.

Junie's mother was small and dainty. Although her daughter resembled her, Junie was already half a head taller than Mrs. Flockhart.

After making Nancy feel very much at home in the roomy, comfortable house, which was furnished with beautiful antique furniture, Mr.

Flockhart tweaked Junie's chin. "It's high time you got home, young lady," he said. "The lambs are crying for you."

Junie laughed and explained to Nancy that she worked for her father. Her job was to look after the newborn sheep. These were kept in a special barn with individual stalls, so they would not be endangered by other animals.

As the group walked into the living room, Nancy noticed a framed, glass-covered picture hanging over the fireplace mantel. It measured about twelve by twenty inches.

"Is this the mystery picture?" she asked.

"Yes," Mr. Flockhart replied. "Nancy, it's all yours to solve. We've given up."

"But let's not start now," Mrs. Flockhart begged. "Dinner is ready."

After the meal was over, Nancy looked at the parchment paintings again. The first of the four was of a beautiful woman; the second a young man with his back to the viewer. Nancy was intrigued by the third picture. It portrayed a group of angels surrounded by clouds. The figure in the center was holding an infant. The last painting depicted a collision between a steamer and a sailing vessel.

Junie and her father had walked up behind Nancy. "What thoughts are going through your mind, young lady?" Mr. Flockhart asked. "I've never had the pleasure of being this close to a detective in action before. I'd be interested in hearing your ideas."

"I'm afraid I haven't much to offer at the moment," Nancy said. "My first reaction is that the picture tells a story about a family. There was happiness in the beginning, but then tragedy struck. I think there is a connection between the second and last paintings. Perhaps something happened to the man at the time of the accident."

"Do you have an inkling of what the strange message might be?" Junie queried.

"I haven't the faintest notion," the girl detective replied, "but give me a little time. When I'm on a case, the facts are foremost in my mind. I refer to them off and on. My best thinking hours seem to be late at night or early in the morning.

"By the way, Mr. Flockhart, have you met an artist named Vincenzo Caspari, who lives in this area?"

The answer was no, and Junie's father asked why Nancy wanted to know.

"Ned Nickerson thought he might be able to help us," she said.

Mr. Flockhart went to the phone and called the artist. A woman who answered said Mr. Caspari would be out of town for a few days.

"I'll call again," Mr. Flockhart said.

Nancy and Junie were weary from their long ride and retired early. The following morning they dressed in shirts and jeans, had a quick breakfast, then went to the barn where the new-born lambs were. Nancy fell in love with each baby as she came to it.

Suddenly she exclaimed, "Why, here's a pure black one lying down! Isn't he darling?"

The man in charge walked up to the girls, and Junie introduced him as Finney.

"Something happened to this poor little fellow," he reported. "Maybe he got stepped on. Anyway, he can't stand up. I guess we'll have to send him over to the slaughterhouse."

"Not yet," said Junie quickly. "Let me look at him."

She entered the stall. As Nancy and Finney watched her, she manipulated the lamb's legs, massaging them, then rubbing the little animal's body. To the onlookers' amazement the little black lamb stood up and bleated *"Baa!"*

"Well, I'll be—he's gonna be all right!" Finney exclaimed.

"I think he will be," Junie said jubilantly, watching the black lamb closely. Then she explained to Nancy that she had had some training in animal massage.

Nancy had noticed that outside there was a great deal of activity, carts and trucks going in both directions. Most of them contained full-grown sheep. Wishing to watch this part of the operation more closely, she walked out of the barn. Junie followed.

Just then a high-powered car roared around the corner of the barn, put on speed, and headed in the girl's direction. The driver made no attempt to swerve out of their path.

Horrified, Nancy and Junie jumped back against the wall to avoid being hit!

CHAPTER III

Plaintive Bleating

THE big car whizzed past Nancy and Junie, missing them by inches as they braced themselves against the wall of the barn. On the passenger side stood a sassy little dog, who leaned out the window and gave quick staccato barks.

The driver yelled at him, "Shut up!" But the dog paid no attention.

The man stopped abruptly and jumped out of the car. He was short and stocky and had a swarthy complexion. He walked back to the girls, and without a greeting of any sort he said to Junie, "Where's your father?"

Before replying, Junie asked, "What was the idea of almost running us down? We might have been killed!"

When the man ignored her question, she went on, "Mr. Rocco, this is my friend Nancy Drew from River Heights. Nancy, this is a neighbor of ours from across the hill."

Rocco did not acknowledge the introduction. His beady black eyes stared into Nancy's blue ones for a few seconds, then he said, "I've heard your name somewhere. In the papers, maybe? Have you ever been in jail or in some other kind of trouble?"

Nancy was taken aback by this rudeness. She merely said, "No."

Junie squeezed her friend's hand and indicated she was to say no more. She herself addressed the man. "Mr. Rocco, I think my father is at the factory. At least, that's where he usually goes in the morning."

Without another word, the crude visitor turned on his heel, went to his car, and jumped in. He drove off rapidly, his dog still yapping.

Junie said to Nancy, "Isn't he horrid? But we have to be nice to him because he's one of my father's best clients. By the way, would you like to go to the factory and see how parchment is made?"

"Yes, I'd like that very much," Nancy said and the two girls got into the Triple Creek jeep and went off.

As they approached a string of one-story buildings, Junie said, "Some of these places are pretty smelly from the animals. Think you can take it?"

Nancy assured her she could and in any case, she would put up with it in order to learn about parchment making.

The first place was the shearing room. Several men were cutting the thick wool from the sheep's bodies. They were using electric knives, which operated very quickly. Now and then one of the sheep bleated pleadingly and Nancy realized that a knife had gone too close and nipped the skin.

As soon as all the wool had been taken off, the sheep were driven into the next building through a fenced-in alleyway. The girls left the shearing room and walked to the slaughterhouse.

"I see what you mean by smelly," Nancy remarked, holding her nose for a moment. "When Bess and George get here, I'll bet Bess won't come near this place. She not only can't stand bad odors, but she can't watch any living creature being killed."

Before the sheep were slaughtered, they showed great fright and their bleating caused a terrific din in the place. Junie told Nancy that after being killed, the animals were hung up to drain. Nancy nodded silently, not looking too happy.

"I guess you've had enough of this," Junie said understandingly. "Let's go in the next building. That's more civilized!"

Here the skins of the animals were skillfully removed so that the meat underneath would not be damaged. As soon as the carcasses were ready, they were carried to a waiting refrigerated truck.

"From here they go to wholesale meat plants," Junie explained. "My father is not involved with that part of the business."

"Now what happens?" Nancy asked.

"I'll show you how the hides are treated before it is possible to make them into parchment," her friend replied.

In the next building men were busy shaving and scraping the tough hairs from the skins of the sheep.

"When these are ready," Junie said, "the hides will be covered with lime. This is done to absorb excess fat. The next step is to douse the hides in a pure water bath, then hang them up to dry. You can see some of them over there being stretched on frames. This is to make them smooth."

"There's a lot of work involved," Nancy remarked.

"You're right," Junie agreed. And the farm girl made Nancy laugh by reciting an original ditty:

> Junie had a little lamb.
> She kept it in a stall.
> But Daddy took the lamb away;
> Now it's a parchment on her wall.

"Junie, you're a great poet!" Nancy said. "Let's see if I can do as well. Nancy thought for a few seconds, and then she recited a rhyme of her own:

> Junie had a little lamb.
> It really got her goat
> When Daddy took the pet away
> And made her friend a sheepskin coat!

"Very clever!" Junie praised. "We're so good we should go in the poetry business."

"Not so fast, partner," Nancy cautioned. "First we will have to solve the mystery of your father's parchment."

"Righto. Well, back to my duties as a guide. The last process in making parchment is again scraping the hides and then sandpapering them. By that time they will look like your father's diplomas."

"What if a sheep has real thick skin?" Nancy asked.

"Then it's possible to separate the outer from the inner layers. Very fine vellum is made from the inner layer. That's the most expensive kind of what we normally call writing paper, but it's really not paper at all because it's not made from the wood of trees. Can you imagine going into a fine stationery store and asking for a box of sheepskin to use for letters?"

Nancy chuckled. "Right. The salesclerk would think you'd escaped from a funny farm. By the way, can you make parchment and vellum from other animal hides, too?"

"They use the hides of calves and goats, but they're coarser than sheepskin, so my dad doesn't bother with them."

Nancy said it had been a very interesting and enlightening tour.

"Oh, the sightseeing isn't over yet," Junie replied.

"Really? What else is there to visit?"

"I want you to meet a very interesting character who works for my dad. He has nothing to do with this factory, though. He's an elderly shepherd who lives high on one of our hills and takes care of a large flock of sheep. His name is Ezekiel Shaw, but everyone calls him Eezy. I won't tell you any more about him now, but you'll like him. I have a walkie-talkie in my car for him."

Junie drove the jeep partway up the hill, then parked it. "We'd better walk from here. Sometimes the engine of this jeep disturbs the sheep. They're timid and scare easily."

Almost immediately a beautiful sheep dog came to meet them. "Hello, Rover!" Junie said to him, ruffling his thick fur. "Rover, this is Nancy Drew, who is visiting me. Make her welcome to Triple Creek Farm."

Rover sat down and put up his right paw to shake hands. Nancy responded and patted the dog lightly on the back of his head.

"I'm glad to meet you, Rover," she said. "I take it you guard the sheep."

The dog seemed eager to be off. Junie said he probably felt he should get back to Eezy, his master. The girls followed him as quickly as they could, but could not worm their way among the sheep as easily as the dog did.

Nancy and Junie finally reached the top of the hill. Before them stood a small cabin with trees around it. The place was quiet and well kept.

"Is that where Eezy lives?" Nancy asked.

"Yes. But when the weather is good, as it is today, he's usually outdoors. He must be around here somewhere. Often he's seated on that big rock over there. From that spot he can look all around and see if any of the sheep need attention, or if there are any prowlers."

"What kind of prowlers?" Nancy asked.

"Oh, rustlers who come to steal sheep, or sometimes wild dogs."

Junie began calling Eezy's name. There was no response from the elderly shepherd.

"This is strange," Junie said. "I wonder where he is."

Suddenly Rover began to bark wildly and to zigzag quickly among the sheep. He headed down the slope at a different angle from the direction the girls had taken to come up.

"Let's find out where Rover's going," Junie suggested. "I suspect trouble."

She and Nancy hurried down the hillside. By now all the sheep seemed disturbed. They began to move around, and a few started to run. Had the dog caused this, or was there some other reason?

Far down the hillside the girls could hear both Rover's bark and the sheep's loud bleats.

Junie looked worried. "Now I'm sure there's trouble of some kind down there. We'd better find out what it is—and fast!"

CHAPTER IV

Eezy Shaw

NANCY followed her friend as fast as she could. The sheep were everywhere. Some were standing, others were lying down. In her haste to keep up with Junie, Nancy decided to hurdle some of the animals. Once, while jumping across an old sheep that was lying down, she stepped on the tiny tail of a younger one. Immediately there was a loud *baaaaa.*

"I'm sorry," Nancy called back, as she sped on.

When the girls neared the lower end of the hill, they noticed two men running as fast as they could toward a road at the foot.

"They must have caused the disturbance," Nancy called. She asked, "Do you know who they are?"

"No," Junie replied. "Maybe they were trying to rustle our sheep."

"That's bad," Nancy remarked.

The men were too far ahead for the girls to get a good look at them. Junie said she still did not recognize either one of them. A moment later the two intruders jumped into a waiting car that roared off.

Rover had been after the men, but could only scare them away. When he realized the girls were coming down, he turned and trotted up to their side.

"Good dog!" they both said, and Junie hugged him affectionately. As the three climbed the hill, Nancy asked, "I wonder where Eezy is?"

"I do, too," Junie replied. "It's not like him to leave his station, especially if there's any trouble and the sheep are disturbed."

As soon as the girls reached the top of the hill where Eezy's cabin stood, they began to call the shepherd's name. When there was no answer, Junie went inside the house. He was not there.

Puzzled, she said to Nancy, "I can't imagine what happened." She leaned down to the dog and said, "Rover, where is your master? Go find Eezy. Take us to Eezy."

The beautiful animal cocked his head. Then, as if understanding what was wanted of him, he sniffed along the ground, apparently trying to pick up the scent of Eezy's footprints. Presently he disappeared into a small copse of trees. Meanwhile, the girls looked all around the cabin and some distance beyond it. There was no sign of

Eezy, nor any clue as to what had become of him.

"This is really strange," Junie remarked. "Eezy has never left this place since he became a shepherd here."

At this moment Rover began to bark wildly. Nancy and Junie followed the sound, which led them to an area in the copse of trees. The faithful dog was standing beside his master, who lay stretched out on the ground, unconscious!

"Oh!" the girls cried out and knelt down next to him.

The shepherd was just beginning to revive. He mumbled and presently Nancy caught the words, *"I will seek that which was lost, and bring again that which was driven away."* *

Nancy looked at her friend for an explanation. Junie said that Eezy was a very religious man, who often quoted the Bible to explain the philosophy behind some situation. "I think he's blaming himself, perhaps for letting some of the sheep be rustled."

"It looks as if you and I got here just in time," Nancy said.

Junie nodded and gave the stricken man some first aid to help him regain full consciousness. He did not respond at once, so Junie said, "Nancy, you try it."

Nancy did and in a short while the shepherd

* Ezekiel 34:16

opened his eyes wide, then smiled wanly. Finally, with their help, he got to his feet.

"This is no kind of reception at all," the slender, elderly man said. "And, Junie, I see you've brought a beautiful young lady to meet me."

"Yes, this is my friend Nancy Drew," Junie told him.

"Sorry I was sleepin' when you came up," Eezy said. "Next time I'll be wide awake, I promise."

The girls looked at each other, then Junie said, "Eezy, you were not just asleep. You were unconscious. What happened to you?"

The shepherd hung his head. "I see I can't keep anythin' from you. Well, two men came up here to see me. We didn't quite hit it off. They got mad and knocked me out. Never gave me a chance to fight back."

Nancy explained that she and Junie had seen two men running very fast down the hill with Rover after them.

"But," Junie added, "before we got close enough to identify them and see their license plate, they sped away in a car."

"That's just as well," Eezy said. "They're tough, bad people. Take my word for it. And don't get involved with 'em."

Junie begged the elderly shepherd to tell them why the men had been there. Eezy shook his head. "I'm not goin' to say anything more about 'em 'cept that they wanted me to do somethin' I don't approve of. We had just better let it go at that."

By now Eezy seemed to have recovered his strength, and he walked back with the girls to his cabin. "May I invite you lovely ladies to join me in a glass of cool lemonade?" he asked. "This is the time of day I like to wet my whistle."

Nancy and Junie accepted and followed the shepherd inside. The place was immaculate and attractively decorated with furniture Eezy had made. He was pleased that the girls were interested in his handicraft.

He did not refer to the unfortunate incident, except to say that he was mighty thankful to Rover for having run the men off the premises.

Nancy asked, "Where was Rover when the men were here?"

"I think he was off chasin' a wild dog, maybe. I heard another dog bark."

"I have something for you in the jeep," Junie said. "My father asked me yesterday to bring you a walkie-talkie. If you have any more unwanted visitors here, just call the farmhouse and reinforcements will come at once to help you."

"That's very kind of you," Eezy said. "I hope I won't have to use it."

As the girls walked to the car to get the instrument, Junie said, "It's too bad Eezy didn't have the walkie-talkie sooner."

"I wonder if he would have had a chance to use

it," Nancy said. "Obviously he talked to the men first, but didn't realize they would beat him up."

Junie nodded. "Now that he knows, he can call if he sees them in the distance."

When the girls returned to the cabin, Junie showed the shepherd how to use the walkie-talkie.

Eezy's eyes twinkled. "I can call you now and ask you to come up and keep me company!"

"You do that," Junie said, then the girls bid him good-by. On the way home they discussed the incident.

"Have you any idea what the men could have wanted that Eezy didn't approve of?" Nancy asked.

"Not the slightest," her friend replied. "Of course, I suspect that they might have been trying to bribe him into helping them rustle sheep. But then it might have been something more personal that Eezy didn't want to talk about."

Nancy asked if there was much sheep rustling in the rest of the neighborhood.

"No," Junie replied. "There are only a few sheep farms around here besides Dad's. More than likely, since they had only a car with them and planned to steal sheep, they would have taken only one or two for food."

"Then it's more of a puzzle than ever what they wanted Eezy to do that he wouldn't, and his re-fusal made them so mad they knocked him out."

Junie suggested that perhaps her father might

have some ideas on the subject, so after dinner that evening she asked him. He thought for some time and wrinkled his brow. "I don't like this. There are so many miles of unguarded fields in this area that all kinds of things could happen. The attack on Eezy bothers me. It's too bad you didn't get a better glimpse of those men."

Nancy said they were of medium height and build. Both wore hats pulled far down, so she could not see the color of their hair or their skin.

"Hm," Mr. Flockhart said, "I'll alert the State Police to keep an eye open." He went to the hall telephone to call them.

While he was gone, Nancy stared at the parchment over the mantel. Then she got up and stood beneath it, taking in every detail.

When Mr. Flockhart returned to the room, he said, "I see you have already started looking for clues to solve the mystery of my parchment."

Nancy admitted that she had noticed only one thing so far. She could not find an artist's name on it.

"That's right," he agreed.

"The first picture," Nancy went on, "is of a lovely woman but she's not doing anything to indicate what part she is playing in the message."

"That's true," Mr. Flockhart replied. "What about the second one?"

Nancy studied it for several seconds. "A portrait of the upper part of a man, but a rear view," she said. "All I can see is that he seems stocky and has dark hair. That's not much help."

"No, it isn't."

"The third picture is the most intriguing of all," Nancy went on. "See that group of angels in flowing robes floating in the heavens? And the one in the center is holding an infant. All the others are looking at it adoringly. It's just beautiful. Only a very fine artist could have painted that."

Nancy now concentrated on the fourth painting, the scene of a sailing ship being rammed by a steamer.

"I think it's an accident that really happened," Junie said. "Nancy, what's your guess?"

"I don't know. Perhaps the steamer is wrecking the sailing ship intentionally. I'm sure there's a message here. But what?"

Turning to Mr. Flockhart, she asked, "From whom did you buy this parchment?"

"From my neighbor, Sal Rocco," Junie's father replied.

Nancy instantly remembered the unpleasant man and became very thoughtful. "Did he tell you where he got it?"

"He said he bought it at an auction, but was tired of it and agreed to sell the parchment painting to me."

"Does he know what it means?"

"No. I asked him if there was any story to it, and he said not as far as he knew."

"Have you ever taken this parchment out of its frame?" Nancy went on.

"No," Mr. Flockhart replied. "Why?"

"There might be a message on the back, or at least a clue to one."

"Good idea," Mr. Flockhart said. "Let's take it out right now!"

CHAPTER V

Bird Attack

THE mystery picture was carefully framed, and looked as if it had never been opened. Mr. Flockhart removed the backing, then slid out the parchment. He held it up for the others to see.

"It's even more beautiful out of the frame!" Junie exclaimed.

Mr. Flockhart handed the picture to Nancy, who turned it over.

"Here's an initial," she noted. "It's an A." She flipped the picture over to look at the front again. In a moment she exclaimed, "The A is directly in back of the baby who is being held by the angel!"

Mr. Flockhart said, "I wonder if it has anything to do with St. Anthony."

The others doubted this, and Junie asked, "Is there another notation on the back?"

Nancy looked closely. "Yes, there is," she said,

excited. "In the lower right-hand corner are the initials DB, and under it is printed *Milano*."

"Milano?" Mr. Flockhart repeated. "That must mean Milano, Italy, although there is one in Texas."

Nancy turned to him. "I assume Mr. Rocco is Italian. Perhaps he brought the parchment from Italy."

"That's a logical guess," Mr. Flockhart replied. "He might have bought it at an auction over there." He smiled at Nancy. "I can see why you are known as such a good detective. Just by taking the parchment out of the frame you've come up with a couple of clues already!"

"Oh, don't compliment me now," she answered modestly. "Wait until I've solved the case."

Junie teased, "Your next stop may be Milano!"

"I think we should go and see Mr. Rocco," Nancy said. "He might be able to tell us more."

Junie's father agreed, but said, "Not tonight, please. Wait until morning."

Nancy asked Junie if she knew the way to the Rocco farm. The girl shook her head. "I've never been there. Dad, can you tell us how to get to Mr. Rocco's?"

"Sure," Mr. Flockhart said and gave the girls explicit directions. "As you know," he added, "I don't care for the man. Please be very careful while you're there. He may become suspicious that I'm sending you over to see him with some ulterior motive in mind. I don't want that to happen. After all he is a good customer and I'd hate to lose his business."

Nancy and Junie said they understood and would follow his instructions. Then they went to bed early so they would be well rested for their mission.

The following morning after breakfast they drove to the Rocco Farm. When they arrived, the girls noticed that the house and grounds were surrounded by a high fence. There were two iron gates blocking the entrance.

The friends looked at each other in dismay. "Your father was right," Nancy said. "This man must be suspicious of everyone in the area to barricade himself like this. What a terrible way to live!"

Junie tried to open the gates, but found that they were locked. "Stymied already," she said.

"Here's a bell," Nancy said, pushing the button. "We're not defeated yet. Where there's a will, there's a way!"

The girls waited, but no one came to answer their call. Nancy pressed the button again, holding it firmly in place for several seconds. Still there was no response of any kind.

"I can't imagine that there's no one around," Junie remarked. "Surely there must be someone to come and let us in."

Nancy said that perhaps the owner did not

want any visitors. "Or maybe the bell doesn't work," she added. "Are you game to climb over the fence with me, Junie?"

"Sure."

Since both girls were wearing jeans and shirts, it was not much trouble for them to get over the enclosure. In front of them was a long lane, bordered on both sides by a stone wall.

"Not a very inviting place," Junie remarked, gazing ahead. "Soon we'll see a sign saying, 'Beware of the people who live here. They may bite.' "

Nancy laughed, then said, "Let's keep our eyes and ears open. We don't want to miss anything. Look over there. Several cars are parked near the house. This proves somebody is home. Probably Mr. Rocco is having a very private meeting and doesn't want any outsiders around. That's why he wouldn't answer the bell."

The girls went on. They had almost reached the stone farmhouse when they became aware of great fluttering overhead. Startled, they looked up. The next second a huge flock of black birds descended and attacked the visitors viciously!

"Ouch!" Junie cried out. "That hurts. Get away from me!"

She and Nancy tried hard to fight off their unfriendly attackers. The large birds had long claws and prominent beaks. Each girl put one arm over

The vicious birds attacked Nancy and Junie.

her face and with her free hand tried batting at the birds to make them fly away. But their efforts seemed hopeless, and the battle continued.

Making no headway, Nancy and Junie began to scream as loudly as they could. "Help! Help! Someone please help us!"

Their cries were almost drowned out by the raucous noise made by the birds. No one answered the girls' pleas, so in desperation they dropped to the ground and doubled up, putting their heads and arms under their bodies. This seemed to anger the birds, who made more noise than ever and pecked mercilessly at the helpless visitors.

Once Nancy raised her head and screamed at the top of her lungs. "Help us! Quick! We need help! Hurry!"

Whether it was her cry that was heard by the men in the house or the frightening noise of the birds, the girls did not know. Several men rushed out, yelling. Finally the birds flew off.

One man walked up to Nancy and Junie and asked in an unpleasant, demanding voice, "What are you doing here? Don't you know this is private property?"

Junie explained that her family was a neighbor to Mr. Rocco and they had come to see him on an important matter. "Please take us to him."

"You can't visit him now," the man replied.

"He's in conference. How did you get into the grounds?"

Neither girl answered. They were staring at their interrogator and at the other men who by now had arrived at the scene. All of them looked tough and unfriendly. Rocco's pals resembled underworld characters, Junie and Nancy thought.

"Who owns those birds?" Nancy asked. "Mr. Rocco?"

In a surly voice one of the group replied, "What makes you think anybody owns them? In any case, it's none of your business. What right do you have to ask questions? Now get out of here before you cause any more trouble."

Junie asked him, "Will you please unlock the gate?"

The man squinted at the girls and said, "No, I won't, and neither will anybody else. We've had enough guff from you smart alecks. You got in here; now get out. But don't try any funny stuff, because I'll be watching you!"

With no choice Nancy and Junie hurried down the lane. The man who had ordered them out followed at a distance. He made no move to open the gate, so once more the girls were forced to climb the fence.

Junie then drove toward Triple Creek, but took a road traversing the neighboring village. "Let's stop at the general store and get some ice cream," she said. "All that exercise has made me hungry. Besides, when I get mad I get hot, and something cool will taste good."

The girls went into the store, which included a few tables where customers could eat sandwiches, cookies, and ice cream.

Nancy and Junie sat down. Presently a woman came to wait on them, and after serving heaping saucers of vanilla ice cream topped with whipped cream and pecans, she stopped to talk to them. Junie introduced her as Mrs. Potter, and said she managed the store for a friend. She then told the woman of the girls' recent experience.

"You know Mr. Rocco, don't you?" Junie said. "What can you tell us about him?"

The woman stiffened. "Nothing good," she replied. "Besides, he has some men working for him that I don't like. They were in here one day, talking to me. I couldn't agree with a thing they said. I never want to see them again and I hope from now on they'll all shop in another store."

"Could you tell us why you don't like him?" Junie asked.

"No, I'd rather not. It was something concerning my work, and I don't care to discuss it. Sorry."

The girls respected the woman's wishes and said no more. As soon as they had finished their ice cream, they left the store.

After they were in the car and on the way

home, Nancy asked Junie if Mrs. Potter was always so abrupt.

"Oh, no," Junie replied. "She's a very nice person and usually full of fun. I can't understand why she acted the way she did."

Nancy was silent for a few minutes, then said, "It's my guess she has been intimidated, perhaps by the same men and in the same way that Eezy was!"

CHAPTER VI

"No Speak English!"

LATER, when Nancy thought Mr. Rocco would be free, she called his home. Another man answered and said he would get the owner. Several minutes passed but no one returned to the phone.

"Maybe he had to go a long way to find Mr. Rocco," Nancy reasoned.

A few minutes later, she thought, "It wouldn't surprise me if Mr. Rocco didn't want to talk to me after I climbed his fence!" She could not understand, however, why her call had not been disconnected. Over and over she said into the phone, "Hello? Hello? Hello!"

Finally she heard Mr. Rocco, who was not very cordial. He said, "If you want to see me, I'm glad you called up for an appointment. I don't like people who climb over my fence uninvited!"

Nancy apologized for having done this but

added in a pleading voice, "Junie Flockhart and I were eager to see you. When we thought the bell didn't work, we took a chance. Please forgive us."

"What do you want?" Rocco asked abruptly without acknowledging the apology.

"I have come across some very interesting information that I would like to discuss with you— but not over the phone."

After a moment of silence on the other end of the line, Mr. Rocco said, "You know I am a very busy man."

"Oh, yes," Nancy replied, "but we won't take up very much of your time. Please. We'd like to talk to you as soon as possible."

"How about next week some time?" the man asked.

Nancy's heart sank. Next week! She could not wait that long. "We were hoping that perhaps we could see you tomorrow," she said.

There was another long pause, then Mr. Rocco said, "What's the hurry?"

"I'll be able to tell you that when we get together," Nancy answered. "Couldn't you spare a few minutes tomorrow morning, say at nine o'clock?"

"Nine o'clock! I make my workers get up at six!" the man said.

"Any time you say will be all right with us," Nancy told him.

Mr. Rocco reluctantly agreed to eight o'clock and added, "Don't be late. I can't stand tardiness."

Nancy thanked him and cradled the phone. She went to tell Junie of their early appointment.

"Oh, Mr. Rocco is impossible, just as my father said!" Junie exclaimed. "But we'll be there. In fact, I suggest we arrive at his home by quarter to eight so he won't get mad. By the way, congratulations for persuading him."

Nancy smiled. "It was a bit of a problem, but it worked."

The two agreed to go to bed early in order to awaken in time for their conference.

The following morning they arrived promptly at quarter to eight. In response to the bell the gate swung free. A man opened the door to the house and said he would see if Mr. Rocco had finished his breakfast. Nancy and Junie looked at each other but said nothing. What about Mr. Rocco's bragging that he made his workers get up at six o'clock?

Nancy thought, "He's a bit of a slave driver."

In a few minutes the farm owner appeared. He neither smiled nor shook hands. Instead he growled at them, "I told you not to be late but I didn't want you to come so far ahead of our appointment, either!"

Junie said that the girls would wait until he

was ready. Both she and Nancy felt that this unpleasant man tried to intimidate anyone with whom he came in contact. When Rocco realized that his method did not work on the girls, he scowled and paused for several seconds before replying to his callers.

"You don't have to wait. But be quick about what you want. I haven't much time, you know."

Without hesitation Nancy said, "We are very interested in the parchment you sold to Mr. Flockhart. Did you bring it from Italy?"

"Yes," Rocco replied. "I bought it at an auction there."

"Can you tell us anything about it?" Nancy went on.

"I don't know anything about it. At first I liked the figures painted on the parchment, but a while ago I got tired of looking at them, so I decided to sell the picture. It's very fine work and brought a nice price. I guess Mr. Flockhart recognized a good thing when he saw it."

"The parchment's lovely," Nancy agreed. Then she asked Mr. Rocco if he had ever taken the parchment out of its frame to look for anything of interest that might have been written on the back.

The man stared at his visitors intently. "No," he said. "It never occurred to me. Did you find something?"

The two girls glanced at each other. They thought it best not to tell him what they had discovered.

"Oh, we studied it, but there wasn't much on the back," Nancy said lightly.

Rocco did not inquire just what they had discovered, and the girls were glad. Suddenly the man bombarded them with questions.

"Why this great interest in the parchment? Do you feel there is something wrong with it? Is your father sorry he bought the painting? Does he expect me to buy it back?"

Mr. Rocco paused, but only long enough to catch his breath. "You young whippersnappers come barging into my home and hammer me with questions. What's going on? I think I have a right to know."

By this time the man was very excited, and for a short time Nancy felt guilty about upsetting him. Then she thought of several things that had happened and her attitude changed. She said she was sorry if she and Junie had harassed the farm owner. They meant no harm. Their main interest was to learn the background of the parchment. This seemed to satisfy Mr. Rocco for the time being.

Junie changed the subject and asked Rocco, "Were you ever married?"

"No!" Rocco said quickly, and did not volunteer any more information. Instead, he stood up as if he were afraid Nancy or Junie might ask more questions he did not want to answer. He indicated that the visit was over.

The girls walked to the front door, with Rocco following them stiffly. On the way home in the car, Junie said, "I wonder why Mr. Rocco was so unwilling to give us anything but the barest information about either the parchment or himself."

Nancy said she thought he was a man with many secrets, which he had no intention of divulging.

Junie remarked, "I just think he's an old grouch. How are we going to find out anything about the picture he brought from Italy if he won't talk?"

Nancy thought for a few seconds, then replied. "Let's try to get the information in spite of him! We'll leave the car on the road and hike across the fields until we meet one of his workmen. Maybe he'll talk, and we can learn more about Rocco."

"His first name is Salvatore, by the way," Junie said.

It was several minutes before they saw a man hand hoeing in one of the vegetable fields. The girls went up to him and smiled.

"Good morning," Nancy said.

The man remained silent, though he smiled at her. She wondered if he were deaf, so this time she shouted her "good morning." Still there was no response and the farmer went on working.

Junie walked close to the man and shouted at him, "Do you live here and work for Mr. Rocco?"

The man shrugged. "No speak English," he finally said.

Nancy and Junie looked at each other and walked on. Across the field they saw another worker and headed in his direction. They put the same question to him and received the same answer, "No speak English!"

Junie sighed. "No one around here seems to speak our language. We're getting nowhere fast."

As the girls walked on Nancy suddenly spotted something and pointed. "I see a boy over there. Maybe we'll have better luck with him."

They walked toward the lad, who appeared to be about ten years old. He was handsome with large brown eyes and black curly hair.

The boy was seated on the ground in the shade of a large branch, and was holding a sketching pad and colored pencils. He was drawing a picture of the landscape spread before him. Against a tree nearby stood a hoe.

"That's very good, sonny," Junie told him, looking closely at the sketch. "What is your name?"

The little boy smiled but said nothing.

"Do you speak English?" Nancy asked.

The boy shook his head. "No English. Italian."

Suddenly the young artist jumped up. He hid his sketching pad and pencils under a sweater and grabbed the hoe. He moved off a little distance and began to work furiously. Nancy and Junie looked at him in surprise. Since they made no attempt to move, he pointed in the distance. They followed the direction of his finger. Mr. Rocco was coming toward them at a fast pace!

"We'd better scoot," Junie warned. "I doubt that Mr. Rocco would like our being here."

Nancy nodded and the girls hurried off in the opposite direction. On the way home, Nancy said, "I believe if young Tony could speak English he might give us some clues."

"How do you know the boy's name is Tony?" Junie asked.

Nancy grinned. "I saw it on his sweater!"

"Good observation!" Junie praised. "I didn't even notice his sweater."

As soon as the girls reached the farmhouse, Nancy called her father's office. He was there and asked how she was progressing with the mystery.

"Not very well," she replied. "I need your help."

"Sure thing. What can I do for you?"

"Will you please find out from the Immigration Department all you can about Salvatore Rocco, who came to the United States from Italy about ten years ago?" She told her father all she had learned so far.

"I see you've been busy," he said. "I'll check with Immigration and let you know the answer."

After the call, the girls went to look at the mysterious parchment again. They puzzled over it for some time before Junie asked Nancy if she had come up with any new theories.

Nancy's eyes sparkled. "I have a wild guess!" she said.

CHAPTER VII

A Mean Ram

"I THINK we can assume," Nancy said to Junie, "that Mr. Salvatore Rocco knows more about the parchment than he is telling. The initial A on it could stand for Anthony, and a common nickname for Anthony is Tony."

Junie knit her brows. "Are you trying to say that Tony, the little boy we met on Mr. Rocco's farm, might be the baby in this parchment picture?"

Nancy nodded. "I told you it was a wild guess."

"It sure is," Junie agreed, "but I respect your hunches."

Mr. Flockhart walked into the room and was told Nancy's latest theory. He chuckled, but said he was impressed with the idea. "Nancy, please continue with your suppositions. It sounds like an intriguing story, and the first hypothesis that has been made so far in the mystery of the parchment."

Junie remarked that the man pictured on the parchment, who had his back to the viewer, could be the boy's father. "But why wouldn't he be facing the viewer? Was the artist ashamed of him?"

"That's a possible answer," her father agreed. "On the other hand, maybe the artist just didn't like the person and turned him around so nobody could recognize him." He said to Nancy, "Have you any more guesses?"

"Not yet," she replied, "but I may have after I learn more about little Tony and Mr. Salvatore Rocco."

Mr. Flockhart reminded the girls that it was generally believed in the community that Mr. Rocco was the child's uncle and that the boy's parents had died.

"That gives me an idea," Nancy said. "The last picture on the parchment portrays the collision of a sailing ship and a steamer. Maybe," she added, "Tony's parents were killed in the accident."

"Very reasonable assumption," Mr. Flockhart said. "I wonder if Mr. Rocco legally adopted his nephew."

"I guess," said Junie, "that we'd have to go to Italy to find out." She teased, "Nancy Drew, detective, Milano is getting closer and closer."

Nancy grinned. "Maybe, but I have a hunch

I'll solve the mystery right here at Triple Creek Farm."

Junie and her father looked at their guest, then Junie said, "Nancy Drew, you're holding back one of your hunches, or theories, or wild guesses. Come on, what is it?"

Nancy nodded. "You're right. In the first place, I'm not convinced that Mr. Rocco's story to Mr. Flockhart and to us about buying the painting at an auction is true. I've been thinking of poor Tony. He has so much talent as an artist, and so does the person who made these paintings, whose initials are DB. That person could be a close relative of Tony's. By the way, what's his last name?"

"I don't know," Junie's father replied. "I have always supposed it was Rocco."

Mr. Flockhart said he thought the girls should try to find out what DB stood for. "It might be the initials of the artist, or an art school, or a museum, or even a dealer's initials."

"One thing is sure," Nancy said, "Milano is Milano, Italy, so that's as good a place to start as any, but I guess we can't go there."

Junie's father said, "Leaving the mystery for a moment, Nancy, I have a little favor to ask of you. In your spare moments, try your hand at creating an attractive symbol for Triple Creek Farm. I don't like the one I've been using."

"I'll be glad to try," Nancy replied.

As soon as he left the room, she went to the hall table, where the telephone was, and picked up several sheets of paper and a pencil. Junie watched intently as Nancy made sketch after sketch. The girls laughed at some of them.

"This one looks like a three-legged monkey," Junie remarked. "No offense meant."

"And this one like a broken harp with all the strings missing," Nancy added. "Junie, let's do something else. By the time we come back, maybe my imagination will return. Right now I've run out of ideas for a Triple Creek symbol."

"What would you like to do?" Junie asked.

The girl detective thought they should call on Eezy as soon as Junie finished her chores, with Nancy's help. "Maybe he'll be willing to tell us more about those two men who knocked him out, and also what he knows about Mr. Rocco."

Junie agreed. After two hours of work with the newborn sheep, the girls changed clothes and were ready to set off for the shepherd's cabin.

As before, they drove part of the way, then climbed up the hillside among the sheep. Eezy was there, sitting on a log in front of his little cottage and casting an eye over the hundreds of healthy-looking sheep in his flock.

"Howdy, girls!" he greeted them. "I had a feelin' maybe you'd run up here today. Glad to see you."

When Nancy said, "I hope we're not interrupting your work," the shepherd chuckled and immediately answered. "As it says in the book of Hebrews, *'Be not forgetful to entertain strangers: for thereby some have entertained angels unawares.'* " *

The two girls smiled at the compliment, then Junie said, "I'm not an angel, but I do like to help people. Nancy does too. That's why we're here."

"Eezy," Nancy said, "did the two men who attacked you ever return?"

"No."

She asked him if he was still unwilling to talk about what his attackers wanted him to do for them.

"I'm afraid I am," the shepherd replied. "Sorry, but it might get some innocent people into trouble."

Nancy now asked Eezy to tell them all he knew about Mr. Rocco. The herdsman repeated the story Mr. Flockhart had told, then added, "I don't know anythin' else about the Italian, because he's a man without a civil tongue.

"Not one of his workers can speak English, and somebody told me he pushes them very, very hard in the fields. He overworks his men on the produce farm. Besides, he is often cruel. I understand that sometimes he beats that little boy who lives

* Hebrews 13:2

with him. Rocco says he's his uncle, but I don't believe him. He sure doesn't look like the boy or have his disposition."

"Mr. Rocco beats the boy? How dreadful!" Nancy remarked. "Don't the authorities get after him?"

"Guess not," Eezy replied. "But there's a proverb in the Bible that says, *'The merciful man doeth good to his own soul: but he that is cruel troubleth his own body.'* " *

The girls thought about this and decided the proverb was indeed true. They wondered what punishment might come to Rocco for his cruel and unwarranted actions to others.

At this moment a cute and friendly little lamb came up to the girls and stood patiently waiting for their affection. Both of them leaned down and hugged the young animal.

"You're a cutie all right," said Junie. "I'm going to call you 'Cheerio.' "

"Oh, I hope it won't have to be slaughtered," Nancy said, worried.

Eezy smiled. "I won't recommend it, 'cause the little sheep is a real comfort to me. You know it gets mighty lonely up on this hilltop. This little critter comes and sits by my side and listens to all my woes."

"That's something that shouldn't be changed,"

* Proverbs 11:17

Nancy said. "I suggest you put a sign around Cheerio's neck saying, 'Private Property. I belong to Eezy.' "

The shepherd smiled and said he would like that.

In a few minutes the visitors left and started down the hillside. They had not gone far when Junie called Nancy's attention to a large ram standing close by, silhouetted against the cloudless skyline.

"Sometimes he's mean," Junie said. "We'll avoid him."

The girls kept walking but their eyes were on the ram. He looked at them balefully, tossed his head into the air, then lowered his horns.

"He's going to attack you!" Junie cried out. "Run! Nancy, run! Follow me!"

Both girls sped off like a couple of deer, but the ram was also quick. Nancy and Junie managed to stay ahead of him until, without warning, a strange dog began barking nearby.

"Maybe that will frighten the ram away," Nancy suggested.

Junie said there was not a chance of that happening. "This ram is not afraid of dogs," she explained. "One day I saw him toss a big black one high into the air. He almost killed it!"

Nancy was thinking, "This mustn't happen to me!" and ran faster.

She was finally outdistancing the ram when a

large sheep, frightened by the strange dog, ran directly in front of Nancy. She tried to leap over the broad-backed, woolly animal, but could not make it. The next moment she fell flat!

By now the ram had caught up to her. The next moment Nancy felt his curved horns reach speedily under her body.

Wild thoughts went through the trapped girl's mind. Would the ram toss her into the air as he had the dog?

CHAPTER VIII

The Mystery Boy's Story

As the ram got ready to toss Nancy into the air, a desperate thought came to her on how she might save herself. She reached out to grasp the animal's curved horns, caught one with each hand, and hung on.

The animal, angered, tried again and again to throw the girl off, but she kept her grip on the horns, and braced herself against his body. Nancy swung crazily from side to side but did not lose her hold, as the animal endeavored desperately to shake her off.

After one more try, the ram stood still. Was he exhausted or defeated? No matter what the answer was, Nancy regained her balance and stood up, but kept a wary eye on the unfriendly animal.

Junie came running up. "What a dreadful experience!" she exclaimed. "Oh, Nancy, I'm so sorry."

The ram, though mean, knew Junie and made no attempt to attack her. She gave him a resounding slap and sent him galloping off.

The girls had counted on their luck too soon. The ram had not gone far when he suddenly turned around and made a beeline for the girls, horns lowered. At the same moment a loud commanding voice came to their ears.

"Eezy is using his giant megaphone!" Junie said. "He's chastising the ram."

The command lasted for a few seconds, then the insistent animal started moving forward again. At once the strains of beautiful music could be heard. Nancy looked at Junie, puzzled.

"Eezy plays an Irish harp to calm the sheep," her friend explained. "It has never failed yet to halt fights."

This time was no exception. The ram stopped short, sniffed the air, then lay down. All the other sheep on the hillside that were not already resting slowly dropped to the grass.

"That's remarkable!" Nancy exclaimed. "I'd like to go back and thank Eezy. In a way he saved my life."

"All right," Junie agreed. "I'm sure we'll have no more trouble with that ram. No doubt by this time he knows that you and I and Eezy are friends."

When the girls reached the shepherd's cabin, they found him seated outdoors, strumming his harp. As soon as he finished the number, Nancy complimented him on his playing. "You're like David in the Bible," she said.

The elderly man smiled. "Thank you," he said. "You know it says in the book of Amos, *'Chant to the sound of the harp, and invent to themselves instruments of music, like David.'* " *

The girls nodded and Nancy said, "Your small Irish harp is a good tuneful substitute for David's lyre."

"That's what I decided," Eezy replied. "And to tell the truth, I think I can get a lot more music out of it than David did out of his lyre!" He chuckled.

Nancy thanked him for helping her ward off a second attack by the ram. She begged for an encore of his harp playing. The shepherd obliged, then put down his instrument.

He picked up his megaphone and called out, "Rest period is over, boys and girls. Stand up and get to work!" He winked at the girls. "The sheep's only work is to eat grass!"

Nancy unexpectedly asked Eezy if he had a pad and pencil in the cabin. The shepherd went to get them, and at once Nancy started sketching. In a few minutes she drew three streams with a woolly sheep superimposed over them. Under the sketch Nancy printed TRIPLE CREEK FARM.

* Amos 6:5

"How do you like that as a trademark?" she asked.

"It's great," Junie replied.

"Mighty good work," Eezy added. "And it's real picturesque."

Nancy said she hoped Mr. Flockhart would like it. She folded the paper and put it into her pocket. Then she and Junie said good-by to the shepherd and walked down the hill toward the car.

As it carried them toward Triple Creek, Nancy asked, "Junie, do you know anyone around here who speaks Italian?"

Junie said she knew no one in the immediate vicinity, but that her boyfriend, Dan White, was studying Italian at a nearby university. "Why do you ask?"

Nancy replied, "Would he be willing to come here and secretly talk with some of Mr. Rocco's farm workers?"

Junie laughed. "There goes that detective mind of yours again," she said. "I'm sure Dan would love the assignment. I'll try to get him on the phone as soon as we reach home."

Fortunately Dan was in his room, studying. When Junie gave him the message, he expressed surprise. "If you think I can speak the language well enough, I'll be over. I'd certainly like to try acting as interpreter."

It was arranged that he would arrive the next morning around ten o'clock, since he had no classes at that time. Nancy liked him. The tall, red-haired young man was intelligent looking and had a great sense of humor. He was intrigued to hear that Nancy was a girl detective.

"Junie didn't mention this to me," he said. "I'll never be able to match you in tracking down clues."

Nancy grinned. "You won't find that hard."

Dan asked for instructions on the part he was to play. Nancy started by telling him they were becoming more suspicious each day of Mr. Rocco, who seemed to be carrying out some wicked scheme in the area and mistreating the little boy he said was his nephew. "Besides, we're sure that the parchment hanging over the mantel, which Mr. Flockhart bought from Mr. Rocco, holds some special significance. If we could discover the meaning of it, we might solve a couple of mysteries."

Dan asked, "What makes you suspicious of Mr. Rocco?"

Junie told him about the insolent men who had talked to Mrs. Potter at the store; how Eezy was attacked by two strangers who, they suspected, were henchmen of Rocco's; of his reported cruelty to little Tony; and about his unwillingness to permit visitors onto his grounds or into his home.

"Sounds complicated to me," Dan said. "But if I can do anything to help unravel the mystery, I'll be at your service. Shall we go to the Rocco farm at once?"

"Oh yes," Nancy replied. "All right with you, Junie?"

"You bet."

The three set off. Junie took a route that led them through the small nearby village. She pointed out the general store and said, "That's one of our clues!"

Nancy told Dan that she thought clue number two was about four miles away. When they reached the area, Junie turned down a side road.

"I think it best if we are not seen near the gate or the Rocco house," she said. "I'll park down here, under some trees, and we'll walk across the fields until we locate the workmen."

As they started off, hoping to find the Italian laborers, Dan and the girls found most of the terrain hilly. It was a long trek before they saw the first workman. The three detectives walked up to him. Dan smiled and said good morning in English, but the man did not reply, nor even smile. Were these Rocco's orders?

"Try it in Italian," Junie urged Dan.

He did so, but the man shook his head. Puzzled, Dan said a few more things to him. Finally the laborer answered but hopelessly Dan threw up his hands. "This man speaks one of the dialects used in Italy, but he doesn't understand my college Italian, and I don't understand his regional Italian."

The three visitors said good-by, although they knew the listener did not understand them, and went on.

Nancy said, "I see another man way over at the end of this field."

The three trekkers headed in that direction. After a long walk in the hot sun, they reached the farmer's side. Once more Dan tried his college Italian. All he received in reply was a blank stare.

"This is maddening," Junie burst out.

The workman went on with his hoeing. In a last desperate attempt to get some information, Dan said several things to him in the Italian he knew. The laborer merely shook his head.

"I guess we'll have to give up," Dan said. "I'm terribly sorry."

"Let's make one more try," Nancy suggested. "It's possible these men are under orders from Rocco not to talk."

"There's no one else in sight," Junie Flockhart pointed out.

"That's true," Nancy replied, "but how about little Tony?"

Both Dan and Junie felt they had nothing to lose by trying, so the three set off across the field.

It was a long walk to where the little boy was at work. This time he was busy with a hoe. His drawing pad and pencils were not in sight.

As the visitors arrived, Tony politely stopped working and bowed. At once Dan said to him in his college Italian, "Good morning!"

Tony replied, a great smile breaking over his face. Then, as he and Dan talked, Junie's friend translated. "Tony says he is an orphan and that Mr. Rocco is his uncle, but that he has to work very hard and has no chance to play.

"Tony tells me he loves to draw but has to do this on the sly. After you girls were here the other day, his uncle caught him and tore up a drawing pad one of the men had given him secretly. Rocco even burned the pencils."

Nancy was furious. There was no doubt that the boy had great talent. It was shameful that the tools for his art should have been destroyed!

Dan translated further. "After Tony's parents died, he was brought to this country as a baby. He has been reared by Italians from Rome and never allowed to mingle with anyone else. He has had good schooling, but only from an Italian college tutor who comes in the evening. Poor Tony says he is so tired sometimes from working hard all day that the print blurs before his eyes."

Dan went on to explain that Tony had never been away from the farm since the day he was brought there. "His uncle says that some day, when they get rich, the two of them will return to Italy."

Further conversation was interrupted when Tony cried out and spoke excitedly in Italian. Dan translated, "Run fast! My uncle is coming! He will be very angry! He doesn't like trespassers and may harm you. But come to see me again. Oh, please come to see me again!"

CHAPTER IX

Midnight Thief

Tony started working furiously with his hoe and the visitors left quickly, running toward a nearby downhill slope so they would not be seen.

But it was too late. From not far away came a loud shout. Angry words were hurled at them in English, and at Tony in Italian.

"Get out of here! I told you to stay away from this farm!"

Everyone turned to look. Rocco kept yelling. "You girls got no business here! Don't come back or you'll get hurt!"

So Rocco had recognized Nancy and Junie.

Without waiting to be caught by Mr. Rocco, Nancy and her friends fled down the hillside. They reached the car, jumped in, and sped off.

It was not until then that anyone spoke. Dan asked, "What are you going to do now?"

Nancy thought for a few moments while she

caught her breath, and finally said, "I believe I should get in touch with Mr. Vincenzo Caspari. He should be home by now."

"Who is he?" Dan asked.

"An acquaintance of my friend Ned Nickerson," the young sleuth replied. "Ned gave me his address over the phone and thought perhaps he could help us. He's a well-known painter."

Junie and Dan thought this would be a good idea. Nancy went on to tell them that the man had been born in America but his parents had come from Italy. "No doubt Mr. Caspari speaks Italian. I understand he studied in Italy for several years."

Dan grinned. "He probably speaks better Italian than I do! Perhaps he should talk to little Tony."

"I think," said Nancy, "that you did very well and got a lot of important information for us."

"I'll tell that to my Italian professor," Dan replied. "Maybe he'll give me a better grade!"

The university student said he must leave in order to attend a class later that day. He promised to return soon. "Call me if you need me," he added.

As soon as he had gone, Nancy went to the phone and called Vincenzo Caspari. She introduced herself and said Ned Nickerson had suggested that perhaps the artist could help her solve a mystery posed by a puzzling group of pictures on a parchment. "They're supposed to contain a great secret," she concluded.

"That sounds most intriguing," the artist replied. "Ned has told me that you like to solve mysteries. I presume there is more to this story than you're telling me."

"Oh, yes," Nancy replied.

But before she could go on, the man interjected, "I can't imagine how I might be able to help you. When I look at a picture, that is all I see—the composition, the color. I do not look for anything beyond that. It is up to the artist who painted it to reveal whatever hidden meanings he intended."

"Please, Mr. Caspari," Nancy said, "don't say no until you've seen the parchment. I have no real proof my guesses are correct, but perhaps after you see the pictures, you can give me some clues that will help solve the mystery."

"You flatter me," Vincenzo Caspari said. "After all, I am only an artist, not a detective."

Nancy said quickly, "You may find yourself becoming a sleuth before you know it!"

They exchanged a few more words before the artist consented to meet with the young detective. Nancy inquired if it would be possible for him to come over some time soon.

He replied, "I can make it tomorrow morning. Is that soon enough?"

"It would be wonderful," Nancy told him. "What time shall we say?"

Ten o'clock was decided upon. The conversation ceased, and the artist hung up. Nancy did too, but she stood there, deep in thought. Finally she was interrupted by Junie, who was going outside to do some work.

"I want to see if that little fellow whose legs I massaged is getting along all right," she said. "How about coming with me?"

Nancy was glad to. She had been wondering about the little black lamb herself. The girls hurried out to the barn where he was kept.

"I see several new lambs have been brought in since yesterday," Junie remarked. "Oh, and here are twins."

Two snow-white bundles of fur lay sound asleep together. Their mother stood nearby. The ewe looked at the girls with a warning eye.

Junie laughed. "I'm not going to hurt your babies. I just want to congratulate you." The ewe seemed to understand and gave a loud *baa*.

"They are darling!" Nancy remarked. "Don't tell me they're likely to be taken away and their skins made into parchment or vellum."

Junie put a hand on Nancy's arm. "That's for my father to decide. After all, this is his livelihood, and business is business."

Nancy realized how necessary the slaughtering

of domesticated sheep, cows, goats, and hogs was. Otherwise the countryside would be overrun with animals. She also thought, "As long as people want to eat meat, this practice will go on."

In a few moments they reached the pen where the injured black lamb was. Both Nancy and Junie were delighted to see that he was walking around quite normally. They plucked some freshly cut hay from a nearby cart and held it for him to munch. He took it gratefully, then looked at the girls with his bright eyes as if asking for more.

Junie laughed. "You didn't know that I was trying an experiment on you," she said. "I just wanted to see if you had a good appetite and could swallow all right." She turned to Nancy, "I think I'll have to report that this little fellow is ready to be put out in a field." She went to a book fastened with a cord to a small desk and wrote down her report.

After lunch Junie got the jeep and the girls rode all around the farm. This time Nancy had a chance to see other large fields of sheep. Each one had a shepherd.

"Eezy is my favorite of them all," Junie told her friend.

The day wore on and Nancy could not help thinking how quickly it had gone by, when Junie reminded her it was time to go to bed. All the lights were extinguished and everyone went upstairs. In a short time the house became very quiet.

Junie fell asleep at once, but Nancy lay awake, going over the whole mystery in her mind. Each time her thoughts would lead to Tony. She became incensed at Mr. Rocco and thought, "He might cause a permanent injury to that boy! Tony should be taken away from him!"

Presently Nancy became fidgety. Not only was she wide awake, but questions were going round and round in her head.

"It's no use staying here," the girl detective told herself finally. "I'll go downstairs and study the parchment for a while."

Nancy put on her robe and slippers, picked up her flashlight, and tiptoed from the room. She closed the door and walked softly along the hallway to the stairs, descending noiselessly so as not to awaken anyone. Then she crossed the big hall.

Nancy was about to turn on a light switch, when she was startled by a thin shaft of light moving across the living room. She saw no one, but realized that it was impossible for the light to move by itself.

She strained her eyes and finally discerned the dim figure of a man holding a flashlight. Presently the light stopped moving and was beamed directly on the parchment hanging over the mantel.

Nancy's heart was beating very fast. Was some member of the household holding the flash? Suddenly she realized he was an intruder. The man was wearing a stocking mask!

The girl sleuth stood perfectly still, hardly daring to breathe. Suddenly the masked figure reached up and took down the picture.

Nancy decided it was time to act. "Leave that alone!" she commanded.

In response the man turned around and threw the picture at Nancy. It missed her by a fraction of an inch and crashed against the door jamb. It fell to the floor, the glass broken to bits.

Nancy tried to reach the light switch, but before she could do so, her assailant shone his brilliant light directly in her face. She could see nothing!

The thief leaped across the room and grabbed the parchment and frame. He dashed to the front door.

"Stop! Stop!" Nancy cried at the top of her voice.

As the intruder started to open the front door, Nancy reached him. He tried to ward her off with his free hand, but she managed to get hold of it and rip off the glove he was wearing.

The girl's movement had been quick, but it gave the thief a chance to fend her off. With a great shove he sent her reeling across the hallway. As she was regaining her balance, the man opened the door and rushed out, carrying the precious parchment with him!

"Leave that alone!" Nancy commanded.

Just as Nancy recovered her wits, the house was flooded with lights. Mr. and Mrs. Flockhart and Junie hurried down the stairs, each asking what had happened. Nancy quickly explained. At once Junie's father set off an earsplitting alarm. He explained that it would awaken the workers in their cottages so they would be on the lookout for the burglar.

Mrs. Flockhart said, "Shouldn't we alert the police, also?"

Her husband agreed, so Junie hurried to the phone and called. Meanwhile, Mrs. Flockhart took Nancy into the living room and made her sit down on the couch.

"This was a dreadful experience for you," she said. "Now I want you to take it easy."

The girl detective was much too excited to take it easy. Besides, she felt all right and tried to reassure Junie's mother.

"I'm furious at myself for letting the thief get away!" she said. "That was bad enough, but to think he took the parchment with him!"

Nancy was on the verge of tears. Apparently Mrs. Flockhart realized this. Giving the girl a hug, she said, "I think we should be thankful that you weren't hurt!"

Nancy appreciated the concern and tried to smile, but she said, "I came here at Junie's invitation to solve the mystery of the paintings on that parchment. I didn't do it and now the parchment is gone! I may as well go home," she finished with a sigh.

"Oh, no, no!" Junie's mother said, holding Nancy tighter. "I'm sure my husband and daughter wouldn't hear of such a thing. As a matter of fact, Nancy, now you have a double mystery to solve. You must first find the parchment and then tell us its meaning."

CHAPTER X

Running Footprints

For a while Nancy and Mrs. Flockhart wondered who the parchment thief might have been.

"Have you any ideas at all?" the woman asked the girl detective when they came to no conclusion.

"No, not really," she replied. "Of course I think our first idea would be Mr. Rocco, but the man who was here was too tall."

"Anyway," said Mrs. Flockhart, "why should Mr. Rocco feel he had to steal the parchment? All he had to do was come and ask Mr. Flockhart to sell it back to him."

"That's true," Nancy agreed. "But I think Mr. Rocco became worried after I quizzed him about the pictures. Buying back the parchment might make it too obvious that he wanted it, so he had someone take it."

"That's good reasoning," Mrs. Flockhart said.

"On the other hand, a person who knows the true story of the parchment may have stolen it, and will do some blackmailing."

At this moment Mr. Flockhart and Junie walked in with a State Policeman. They all sat down together in the living room.

"Any luck?" Mrs. Flockhart asked her husband.

He shook his head, then introduced the State Policeman, Officer Browning. Mr. Flockhart said that his chase and that of the police and the many workers on Triple Creek Farm had yielded no sign of the fugitive.

"It is unfortunate," the officer said. "We'll have to hunt for clues."

Nancy produced the glove she had torn from the thief's hand and gave it to the officer. "I grabbed this from the burglar's left hand," she explained.

"This is an excellent clue," Browning said. When he was told by Junie that Nancy was an amateur detective, he asked her, "What is your guess as to the kind of glove it is?"

The young sleuth was flattered and not a bit dismayed. She replied, "It's not a workman's glove. Therefore, I doubt that it belongs either to a sheepherder or to a farmer of any kind."

Officer Browning nodded. "You're right. This could mean that the thief is a professional burglar who is not native to these parts. He may even be from the city."

Junie spoke. "Then it may be very difficult to find him," she said. "Like looking for a raindrop in a pond."

"Not necessarily," the officer told her. "The man could have been hired to do this job and may still be in the neighborhood, delivering it."

He told the others that he would take the glove to the police laboratory and have it thoroughly examined.

Nancy asked, "Can you find clear fingerprints inside the glove?"

The officer shook his head. "No, because the material is textured and porous. But we may get some clue from the glove."

He asked if anyone had touched the front door since the burglar had had his bare hand on it. No one had, so Browning said he would get a fingerprint kit from his car and try to take impressions of the newest set of fingerprints.

Although Nancy had watched fingerprint work by police many times, she never tired of looking at the process. But presently she walked outside. Her eyes picked up a clear imprint of half a shoe. Nancy hurried over to look at it, crouched down, and studied the print intently. Then she got up and looked for another. Using her flashlight, she discovered a series of similar ones for left and right feet in turn. They led across a field to a road. Here the prints ended, and Nancy assumed from tracks in the pavement dust that the thief had gone off in a car.

Nancy quickly returned to the house. By this time the officer had finished his fingerprint work. She asked him to come over and look at the shoe marks. Nancy told him she believed they belonged to the burglar.

"Since they are only of the front half of each foot, they were made by someone running."

Officer Browning nodded. "You're absolutely right, Miss Detective. Now tell me, what kind of shoes was the man wearing?"

"Sneakers," Nancy responded promptly.

The State Policeman shook his head. "You sure know your stuff." he said, "I won't tease you any more. I'll just continue to ask your help."

Junie, who had been indoors, heard the last few remarks and at once told the officer that Nancy Drew had a fine reputation for solving the most difficult mysteries imaginable.

"Oh, stop bragging about me," Nancy pleaded with her friend. She explained to the officer, "I came here to find the meaning of four paintings on the parchment that was stolen, and now it's gone. I've botched the case."

Junie said, "Officer Browning, Nancy says she might go home because she hasn't solved the mystery. Can't you do something to make her stay?"

The husky-looking man smiled. "I tell you what, Nancy. Suppose I find the parchment for you; then you can keep the job of solving the mystery of the paintings."

At once Nancy's old eagerness to win the case returned. She said, "I wish you the best of luck and try to make it soon. I can't stay here much longer; I will wear out my welcome!"

The officer got a camera and took pictures of the footprints. Finally he stepped into his car and drove off.

Junie turned to Nancy. "Maybe, just maybe," she said, as she locked arms with her friend and went into the house, "maybe you'll solve both parts of this mystery yourself before the police do!"

Before the girl detective could reply, Mr. Flockhart ordered everyone back to bed. He put out the lights and followed the others upstairs.

Nancy was up early the next day, hunting for further clues to the intruder. First she searched the living room, dining room, and kitchen thoroughly. She could find nothing to indicate how the burglar had gained admittance to the house. She felt he must be a professional with a master key.

Next Nancy went outdoors and again looked at the running footsteps. Satisfied that this was the only clue outside the house, she returned indoors.

The Flockharts were there and they all sat down to breakfast.

Nancy had nearly finished eating, when suddenly she said, "Oh!"

"What's the matter, dear?" Mrs. Flockhart asked.

Nancy said she had just remembered that Mr. Vincenzo Caspari was coming to look at the parchment. "And the parchment is not here!"

Junie suggested that Nancy go at once to call the man so he would not make the trip in vain. Nancy hurried to the phone and dialed the artist's number. A woman answered. When Nancy asked for Mr. Caspari, she was told that he had already left. The young detective, worried, came back to report this to the others at the table.

"That's too bad," Mrs. Flockhart said. "What will you do?"

Nancy thought a moment, then said, "I'll try to make a sketch of the paintings on the parchment as nearly as I remember them. You can help. I'll recite what I know and you add to it."

She described the first picture of a beautiful woman. "I hope I can make her look as much like the original as possible."

Junie spoke up, saying the woman had shiny coal-black hair, large brown eyes with long lashes, a rosebud-shaped mouth, and a lovely olive complexion.

"That's absolutely right," Nancy agreed. "Besides, she had a sad smile."

The others nodded and she went on to mention the man with his back to the viewer, the cluster of angels with one of them holding a baby, and the collision of a sailboat and a steamer.

Mr. Flockhart laughed. "You don't need our help," he said. "Now scoot upstairs and draw the pictures before your guest comes."

"But what if I don't finish them in time?" Nancy replied, worried.

"Don't get so uptight. Just relax," Junie said. "If he arrives while you're upstairs, Dad and I will talk to him."

Nancy darted to the stairs, then stopped. "I don't have any paper or colored pencils with me."

Without saying a word, her friend left briefly and returned with a large, unlined pad and a box of crayons. "Sorry I can't supply pencils."

"Thanks," Nancy said, then hastened to her room. She took a deep sigh as she stared at the blank sheet before her. Then, as if the images on the parchment had suddenly flooded her memory, she began to draw them.

In about twenty minutes she had finished rough sketches of the four paintings. Then, on the back of the one with the baby in it, she printed an A. In the lower lefthand corner of the sheet she put in the initials DB and under it the word Milano.

Nancy had just finished when she heard a car

drive in. She looked out the window to be sure that the person arriving was Mr. Caspari.

The man who alighted was in his forties and was alone. Was he the great Vincenzo Caspari?

Before Nancy could decide, she noticed something that horrified her. The man's car had begun to roll slowly. If it kept going it would crash into a tree!

CHAPTER XI

A Tough Suspect

TAKING two steps at a time, Nancy leaped down the stairway of the Flockhart farmhouse and raced out the front door. Could she stop the rolling car before it crashed into the tree?

The owner, who seemed to be unaware of what was happening, was walking toward the house. Nancy passed him in a flash. He turned to find out why she was in such a hurry, then gasped at what he saw.

Fortunately, his big car was rolling slowly. It had not yet gathered momentum. Nancy was able to yank the front door open, jump in, and jam on the brake. The automobile stopped within an inch of the tree.

"Oh thank you, thank you!" the man exclaimed, catching up to the car. "I am so sorry to have caused you all this trouble." He spoke with an Italian accent.

"I'm glad I saw the car moving," Nancy said. "By any chance, are you Mr. Caspari?"

"*Si, si,*" the middle-aged man replied, bowing slightly. "And you are Miss Nancy Drew?"

"Yes, I am," she answered, stepping from the car, with his assistance. The two walked toward the open front door of the farmhouse.

The artist was a charming person, but by his own admission, a bit forgetful. "I should have remembered to put on the brake," he said.

Nancy merely smiled and made no comment. She led her visitor into the living room and they sat down.

"I tried to reach you on the phone this morning, but was told you had already left your house," she said. "I have a horrible confession to make to you."

"Confession?" Mr. Caspari repeated. "You do not seem like the kind of girl who would have to make confessions."

Nancy made no response to this. "I'll get right to the point," she said. "The parchment that I asked you to come and look at was stolen last night!"

"Stolen?" he repeated. "From this house?"

"From right above that fireplace mantel," Nancy explained.

She told him the whole story, then said that she had attempted to draw something that looked like the original. "I'll show it to you. Perhaps you can give us a clue to the painter of the original."

She excused herself and went upstairs to get the drawing. After she came down and handed it to the artist, he studied the front of the paper for a long time. He even turned it upside down, but quickly put it back into position.

Finally he looked up and said to Nancy, "Did you draw this from memory?" When she said yes, he went on, "It is an excellent drawing, especially the picture of the angels with the baby."

Nancy thanked him and said, "Maybe that's because I think it may be the most significant picture in the group. I'll show you why I think so." She turned the paper over and pointed out that the printed A on it was directly behind the picture of the angels. "This is just the way it was on the original."

The artist rubbed his chin. "And none of the other pictures had initials in back of them?"

"No."

Mr. Caspari told Nancy, "I think you are very observing, as an artist should be. Now please tell me what your theory is."

"My guess is that the A stands for Anthony. We met a boy who is an artist. He is the nephew of the man who sold the parchment to Mr. Flockhart," she explained. "It may be a long and wild guess, but I am wondering if by any chance that boy could be this baby. His nickname is Tony."

The artist wanted to know if Nancy had ever questioned the former owner about the picture. She nodded. "I tried to, but didn't get very far. He is very secretive and uncooperative. By the way, do you know him—Salvatore Rocco?"

"No. I never heard of him. Tell me more about the boy."

Nancy explained the situation, and ended by saying that Mr. Rocco had said he knew nothing about the origin of the parchment. He had purchased it at an auction.

"It is an interesting story," Mr. Caspari remarked. "There's a chance, of course, that his story isn't true."

Just then he spotted the initials DB in the corner with the word Milano under them.

"Have you any ideas about what these initials stand for?" he asked Nancy.

"No, I haven't."

Mr. Caspari said that on this point he might be able to help her out. I brought with me a directory of European artists." He took it from a pocket and began turning the pages. "I'll look under the section for Italy and see if we can find a DB in Milano."

Nancy sat watching quietly as the man flipped page after page.

Finally he said, "No one with those initials is listed in Milano, but I see three in Rome. Their addresses are here. Do you want them?"

"Yes. I would like to have them, but does it say anything about the people?"

The artist told her that two of them were men and one a woman. Nancy was thoughtful for several seconds, then remarked, "Another one of my hunches—I have a feeling, because of the style of the painting of the angels and the baby, that the artist may be a woman."

"That's a good deduction," her caller said.

"Mr. Caspari," Nancy continued, "do you think that this Miss or Mrs. DB could have studied in Milano and painted on the parchment when she was there?"

"That's very likely," he agreed.

Reading from his directory, the artist said that the woman's name was Diana Bolardo. Suddenly he snapped his fingers. "I have the perfect solution!" he exclaimed. "My grandparents live in Rome."

Vincenzo Caspari offered to get in touch with them at once. "I'll phone and ask them to try to find Diana Bolardo."

Nancy was thrilled. How she wished she might go to Rome and investigate herself! She realized, however, that this would be expensive and the clue might lead to a dead end.

"I appreciate this great favor," Nancy told the artist, "and I can hardly wait to hear the answer."

The man smiled. "To tell you the truth, I'm

excited to be part of the team trying to solve this mystery."

After Mr. Caspari had left, Junie came in to catch up on the news. After telling her, Nancy said, "Junie, would you drive downtown with me?"

"Of course. But why?"

Nancy told her she thought the person who had smashed the glass in the frame of the parchment picture might have brought the frame to a shop to have the glass replaced. "Or else, he might just have taken the measurements and will put the glass in himself. Let's go first to a hardware shop."

Junie said there were three in town. They would go directly to the best one.

Nancy tried to explain to a salesman what she was trying to find out. He said no one had brought a broken picture in for him to fix, or bought a twelve by twenty inch piece of glass.

Not discouraged, the girls went outside and Junie drove to the next hardware store. As they walked in, Nancy thought this was a likely place for the thief to have brought the parchment picture. One half of the store was devoted to hardware, the other half to pictures and picture framing.

A pleasant woman listened to Nancy's story, but shook her head. No one had brought in any pictures that morning to have new glass put in, and no one had bought a piece of glass to use himself.

"Thank you very much," Nancy said, and the girls walked out.

"There is one place left," Junie said. "It's not very attractive and it's in a shabby part of town, but I believe it's just the kind of place that a thief might go to."

She drove a few blocks until she came to an older section of town. Finally she parked in front of what had once been a house and was now a store. A gaudy sign in the window read: IF YOU CAN'T FIND IT HERE, YOU CAN'T FIND IT ANYWHERE. The two shoppers smiled.

Nancy remarked, "That's a pretty broad claim. I wonder if the owner can live up to it!"

Junie giggled. "If he can, your quest is over."

The interior of the shop was untidy and badly in need of dusting. A middle-aged man came from the rear room, slid behind the counter, and asked what the girls wanted.

Nancy noted that he eyed them up and down, as if he were asking the question, "What are girls like you doing in this part of town?"

Nancy made her request. At first the proprietor shook his head, saying no one had brought in a picture that morning. Then suddenly he added, "Oh, I forgot. A young fellow from town was in to buy some glass."

"What size was it?" Nancy asked quickly.

The man looked at a piece of wrapping paper lying on the counter not far from his telephone. On it was scribbled 12 X 20 inches. He repeated this to the girls.

"That's just the size we're interested in!" Nancy said. "Who was this young man?"

The proprietor said he did not know, and Nancy wondered whether he was telling the truth or covering up for the thief. Acting as if she believed him, she asked, "What did he look like?"

"Oh, he was of medium height and kind of tough looking. I did notice one thing about him, though His right hand had been bandaged as if he'd cut it. I asked him about it. He told me he had injured his hand on some broken glass that he wanted to replace."

Nancy and Junie were exuberant. They were sure they had tracked down the thief! But the question was, where was he?

"You say you don't know him?" Nancy asked the owner again.

The man shook his head. "I've seen him hanging around town with some other tough guys, but I don't know who he is. In fact, I don't want to know who he is."

The girls felt that the least they could do for all this information was to buy a few articles from the shop. Junie selected a small hammer, an awl, and a package of assorted nails. Nancy found a new type of lawn sprinkler and purchased it to take home to her father. As soon as the articles had been wrapped and paid for, she and Junie left the store.

As they got into the car, Junie teased Nancy. "Now I suppose you will ask me to drive around to where the tough guys hang out!"

Nancy smiled and said, "You're wrong this time. Take me to a drugstore in this neighborhood."

She explained that she wanted to find out where the young man with the cut hand bought the bandage he was wearing.

"It's a long chance, I know," she added, "but, Junie, a good detective tracks down every possible little clue."

Junie said she was beginning to see that. "It amazes me how much trouble you have to go to for one itsy-bitsy clue."

The girls went into the drugstore and approached the counter where first-aid accessories were sold. A pleasant woman waited on them. Nancy asked her if a young man had been in that morning to purchase a fresh bandage for a cut hand.

She was elated when the woman said, "Yes, there was. He was in early. Said he had been in a car accident but didn't have to go to a doctor. He could bandage his own hand."

"Do you know who he is?" Nancy asked hopefully.

"Of course I do. He comes in here a lot. His name is Sid Zikes. I'm surprised that girls like you would be interested in trying to find out about him."

Nancy thought it best not to explain her reason. She merely asked where he lived. This time she received an "I don't know" for an answer.

"But I understand he doesn't have a very good reputation," the woman said. "If you aren't aware of that, I think it's my duty to warn you to stay away from him."

"Thank you for the advice," Nancy said, smiling. "Why does he have a bad reputation?"

The woman said she had been told that upon several occasions when there had been a theft in town, young Sid Zikes had suddenly disappeared. "But the funny thing is that after a while he comes back and nothing ever happens to him. I guess he has been suspected many times but never arrested."

Nancy asked the woman if Sid Zikes ever wore gloves. She said she did not know. "But it wouldn't surprise me. Sid, in his own flashy way, can be quite a dude."

Both girls thanked the woman for her helpful information. Then they bought some powder and perfume. Nancy decided that hers would go to Hannah Gruen.

A few minutes later, as the young detectives were driving off, Nancy said, "Junie, I think we should report our suspicions to Officer Browning. Let's stop at State Police headquarters and tell him or at least leave a message for him." He was not there, so Nancy wrote a note to the absent officer.

When she and Junie finally reached home, Mrs. Flockhart met them. After she had kissed the two girls, she said, "Nancy, you are to call home at once. Your father phoned and said he has some very special news for you!"

CHAPTER XII

Telltale Glove

WHEN Mr. Drew answered the phone, he asked how Nancy was, and how she was progressing with the mystery. Hearing that she was very enthusiastic about her work, he added, "Hannah Gruen and I are both very busy and we keep well, but I must say we miss you very much."

He now began to tell her about his interview with the United States Immigration Department. He said they had made a thorough search and could not find a Salvatore Rocco who had come into the United States from Italy about ten years before, with or without the baby he claimed was his nephew. The lawyer said he was sorry he did not have better news for his daughter.

"Oh, I'm not discouraged," Nancy assured him quickly. "I assume that Mr. Rocco either sneaked into the country with the baby, or came here under an assumed name."

"No doubt you're right," her father agreed, "and it would be almost hopeless to track down this man under such circumstances. But let me know if you get any more clues I can help with," he added.

Nancy now brought him up-to-date on the mystery and ended by telling him about Diana Bolardo. "Do you think it would be a good idea to find out if anyone by that name entered this country either to stay or to visit during the past ten years?"

The lawyer thought it was a good idea. "However, if the woman is living in Rome, it won't be necessary."

Nancy said she would let her father know the instant Mr. Caspari told her what his grandparents had found out.

"And now," Mr. Drew said, "I have a surprise for you. The police caught the girl who stole your jacket."

"Really? How wonderful! What did she say?"

The lawyer reported that the girl had noticed Junie carrying the coat in a see-through bag and felt she had to have it. She followed Junie from the station, found the Drews' door open and tiptoed in. "Her case comes up in two weeks. I guess you'll have to testify against her. Incidentally, she's a known petty thief and hitchhiker. She wasn't acquainted with the man in whose car you saw her."

"Too bad," Nancy said with a sigh.

By the time she had finished her call, Junie had gone outdoors to visit the barn where the new-born lambs were kept. As Nancy sat thinking about the case and what to do next, Mr. Flockhart came in.

"Why so pensive?" he teased. "Did the phone call upset you?"

Nancy told him about the conversation, and then changed the subject. "I was thinking about something else. Would it be possible for me to obtain a piece of parchment the size of the one that was stolen? I'd like to try painting on it to see how close I can come to imitating the four original paintings."

The owner of Triple Creek Farm said he would be glad to let Nancy have a piece of his finest parchment. With a twinkle in his eyes he added, "If you make a really good duplicate of the stolen picture, I'll have it framed and hang it up!"

Nancy grinned. "I don't expect to do anything so wonderful as the original artist did, but I'd like to try. It's just possible it might help us solve the mystery."

Mr. Flockhart said he would take her to the factory at once and choose exactly the right piece. He escorted her outside to his car and they drove off. Since Nancy had never tried painting on parchment, she did not know what to choose, but Mr. Flockhart showed her the different grades of parchment and told her which was the best variety for what she wanted to do.

Nancy thanked him and said she could hardly wait to get started on the painting. She had expected to return home at once, but Mr. Flockhart wanted to speak to Eezy, so they rode back to the house the longer way.

He parked the car where Junie had on previous occasions and walked up the hillside with Nancy. Eezy greeted them with a big grin. The shepherd did not wait to hear any message that might be brought to him.

At once he said, "Howdy, boss! Howdy, Nancy Drew!" Then as he picked up his Irish harp, he quoted from the Bible, " 'Now I can make a joyful noise unto the Lord.' " *

At once he began to accompany himself in a song telling about a lamb that had wandered far from home. Finally though, the little sheep had become so lonesome he could not stand it and turned around and went back. Eventually he rejoined his flock and the ditty ended with a series of *baas* in various pitches.

Nancy and Mr. Flockhart laughed and clapped appreciatively. Nancy now went to pat her favorite lamb, who nudged her affectionately. She noticed that he was growing stronger daily. She had to brace herself to avoid being shoved over.

* Psalm 98:4

In a few minutes Mr. Flockhart finished talking with his herdsman and called to Nancy that he was ready to leave.

"What's the rush?" Eezy asked. "I got somethin' in the cabin I want to show Nancy."

He disappeared inside his shack but soon returned, holding up a glove. The girl detective was amazed. The glove looked exactly like the one she had torn from the hand of the thief who had stolen the parchment painting.

Excited, she asked Eezy, "Where did you get this?"

As the shepherd slipped the glove onto one hand, he said, "You know, this fits perfectly. Rover brought it to me. You're a good detective, Nancy. Do you think you could find me the mate to this?" He began to sing loudly.

Before the callers could answer the question, one of the nearby sheep, apparently unused to his singing, gave a loud *baa*, which made everyone laugh.

It was Nancy's turn to surprise the shepherd. "I think maybe I know where the mate to this glove is. If I'm right, I'll tell you."

Eezy wagged his head from side to side. "You're the most amazing girl I ever met! You take this glove and see if it matches the one you know about."

Nancy now changed the subject and asked Eezy if the two men who had attacked him had ever returned. "I was afraid they might attempt to attack you again."

"Oh, no, nothing like that," the shepherd said emphatically. "I'm keeping that mean ram penned up behind my cabin. If there is any disturbance around here, I'll just turn the old fellow loose on anybody who bothers me!"

"That's a good idea," Mr. Flockhart said.

Nancy was thinking of the walkie-talkie that she and Junie had brought to the shepherd. Apparently he thought the ram would be a quicker and more effective means of warding off an attack!

"And after what happened to me," she thought, "I guess he's right!"

In the meantime Eezy had picked up his harp and began playing a pretty little tune on it. He finished in a few minutes, then Nancy and Mr. Flockhart said good-by and trudged down the hill. When they got into the car, he drove at once to State Police headquarters and turned over the glove Rover had brought to Eezy.

Officer Browning was there and was thunderstruck to see Nancy holding the matching glove.

"There is no question but that this is the mate," he said. "Where did you find it?"

Nancy told him how Rover had picked it up on the Triple Creek property and brought the glove to his master, Eezy.

"I have a strong feeling," Nancy said, "that the thief wanted to get rid of the mate of the telltale glove. He deliberately planted it on Mr. Flockhart's farm to throw suspicion on Eezy or some of the other shepherds or helpers. What do you think, Officer Browning?"

"That you have made a reasonable deduction," he said. "Of course it would be hard to prove, but we may get some other evidence to support your theory."

Mr. Flockhart spoke. "It didn't do that thief a bit of good to try making any of my men look guilty. I trust every one of them, and I am sure all are innocent of any wrongdoing."

The officer nodded. "I would certainly take your word against any other person's," he said. "The police are convinced that the intruder in your home was a stranger, and the theft of the parchment picture was an outside job. Don't worry, there will never be any charge against your men, I'm sure."

After a little more conversation about the mystery, the phone rang, so the visitors stood up to leave.

"Don't go yet," Browning said. "I've been expecting a call. I think it may be of great interest to you."

Nancy and Mr. Flockhart stood still while the officer answered the phone. He said, "Very good. Bring him in here. I have two visitors who would be glad to see him."

The officer put down his phone, but gave no

explanation of the conversation. Nancy and Mr. Flockhart looked at each other, puzzled.

A full minute went by, then the door opened. Two policemen walked in with a handcuffed prisoner. A sullen-looking youth glanced at the visitors, then his eyes dropped.

Officer Browning said, "Mr. Flockhart, Miss Nancy Drew, I want you to meet Sid Zikes!"

CHAPTER XIII

A Paint Disaster

SID Zikes! The young man they had been trying to find! His right hand was still bandaged.

Officer Browning said, "Sid is being charged with petty larceny and will be booked on that count."

Sid Zikes spoke up. "I got a right to bail!"

He was told that this was a judge's decision and he would have to remain behind bars until the amount was decided upon.

The prisoner's eyes roamed from one person to another in the room. Finally they rested on Nancy. The girl detective felt uncomfortable. Was he blaming her for his arrest?

Officer Browning asked Nancy and Mr. Flockhart if they would like to question the prisoner. The sheep-farm owner said he would defer to Nancy. "She knows better than I do what to ask."

Addressing Sid Zikes, the girl detective began.

"Why did you steal the parchment picture from Mr. Flockhart's home?"

Sid looked at the floor and replied, "I didn't."

Nancy told him that she knew he had purchased a new piece of glass exactly the right size to replace the one that had been smashed when he had thrown the picture. The young man made no comment, and looked out a window.

Nancy decided to change her line of questioning. She said, "Did you threaten the shepherd Eezy and knock him out?"

The prisoner shouted, "No!"

"When you went up the hillside to his cabin, who was the person with you? A buddy or a stranger?"

Sid Zikes said definitely, "I don't know what you're talking about, and I don't have to listen to this kind of questioning. Officer, take me away. But I warn every one of you, I won't be in jail long! I'll prove my innocence!"

As Mr. Flockhart and Nancy left State Police headquarters, he said to her, "Do you think Sid Zikes is guilty?"

Nancy replied that she was sure he was the burglar who had taken the parchment picture. "He was about the size and build of the person I caught a glimpse of in your house. But I think it may be true that he had nothing to do with the attack on Eezy."

Mr. Flockhart was inclined to agree. "But I

doubt that Sid Zikes wanted the picture for himself. I believe he was paid by somebody to sneak in and get it."

Nancy asked the Triple Creek owner if he had any guesses about who that person might be. Mr. Flockhart shook his head. "Unfortunately I understand there is a gang in town that will do such jobs for people who would not think of committing the act themselves. So far the police haven't been able to apprehend them."

Nancy remarked, "The person who puts any one up to stealing to gain something for himself is even worse than the thief, don't you think?"

"I agree," Mr. Flockhart said.

He and Nancy went to his car and drove off. She asked him if he would mind going into town so she could purchase some fine colored pencils to make sketches on the parchment.

"I'll be glad to," he said, "but don't ask my advice on the best colors. The truth is, I'm color-blind."

"That's too bad," Nancy said.

The farmer laughed. "It doesn't bother me. So far all my customers who plan to paint on parchment seem to know everything about colors."

After the purchases had been made, Nancy and Mr. Flockhart rode home. He dropped her at the front door of the house, then drove off to his factory.

Junie and her mother were there and were

amazed to hear the story of Sid Zikes's capture and imprisonment.

"I'd say the police are very efficient," Mrs. Flockhart remarked.

Junie spoke up. "But Nancy had some excellent information to give them."

Nancy brushed aside the compliment and asked where she might work on the parchment. "I'm eager to get started," she said.

Junie's mother said she knew the perfect spot. "At the rear of the garden behind the farmhouse there's a lovely summer house. It's an attractive little place. I think you'll like the nice, shady spot. It's quiet and nobody will disturb you."

Junie offered to get an easel from the attic and bring it downstairs. The two girls walked out to the summer house and set up the easel. Nancy got out her colored pencils. Next she stretched the parchment across a frame and pinned it tightly. Then she set it on the easel and said, "I guess I'm ready to start."

Junie watched as her friend meticulously began her work.

The girl artist thought, "I'll do the hardest thing first. That will be the sketch of the beautiful young woman."

She closed her eyes for several seconds, so that she might recall the original picture exactly. Finally she opened them and began to paint.

Junie watched Nancy for several minutes, fascinated, then said she must do her own chores. "I'll be back as soon as possible," she told Nancy.

The young sleuth worked diligently for some time. Secretly she was pleased with the result of her work. "It really does look like the original," she thought.

Nancy had told no one, but what she had in mind was making a parchment picture resembling the original so closely that Mr. Flockhart would indeed want to hang it over the fireplace in the living room.

She smiled to herself. "Maybe I have nerve even to try to do this, but I'll attempt it anyway."

By the time Junie returned, Nancy had almost completed the entire group of pictures. She was working on the sketch of the collision between the sailing ship and the steamer.

Junie was astounded. "Nancy, that's simply marvelous!" she exclaimed.

The words were hardly out of her mouth when the girls became aware of something sailing through the air behind them. The next instant their heads and the parchment were covered with paint!

Nancy and Junie had turned quickly. They were just in time to see two shadowy figures throw down cans of paint and run away. All thought of trying to follow the two men vanished from the girls' minds. The paint was running down from their hair, and they did not dare let it get into their eyes.

Both of them picked up pieces of cloth, which Nancy had handy to use for her work. They wiped off their spattered faces as best they could and then tried to remove the paint from their hair. In seconds they had used up all the available cloths and decided they had better hurry into the house to finish the job.

Nancy paused a moment, however, to look at the parchment. It was ruined! She was on the verge of tears as she picked up the parchment and colored pencils, and followed Junie to the house.

Mrs. Flockhart was near the door when the girls rushed in. She cried out, "What in the world happened to you?"

Junie explained and together they opened a kitchen drawer and took out a roll of cheesecloth. Mrs. Flockhart quickly cut it into sections and handed pieces to the girls. While they worked on their hair, she mopped the paint off their clothing.

"We'd better shampoo right away," Junie advised.

"That won't get off all the paint," her mother said. "It has an oil base. What you should use is paint thinner. Wait here while I run out to the garage for some. I know there's a large can of it there."

She was gone only a couple of minutes. When

The girls' heads were covered with paint!

she returned, Mrs. Flockhart told the two girls to lean their foreheads against the rim of the sink and let their hair fall inside. Then she poured out the paint thinner, and in a little while the combination of the red and blue splotches had vanished.

"Now go upstairs and take hot showers and shampoos," she said.

The girls went to the second floor and reappeared an hour later, looking as if nothing had happened to them. Meanwhile Mrs. Flockhart had tried to remove the paint from the parchment, but had found it impossible. The blue and red liquids had mingled with Nancy's sketches to such an extent that there was no chance of separating them.

"I'm dreadfully sorry this happened," the distressed woman said. "Did you girls see who threw the paint?"

Nancy replied that they had had a glimpse of two figures, but did not see the intruders clearly enough to identify them.

Suddenly she had an idea. "Junie, do you recall that those men threw down their cans of paint?"

"No, all I remember is wanting to get away from them as fast as possible."

"Well, it seems to me they did leave those containers behind. Maybe we can find some clue to where they came from—a brand name or some other kind of identification. Let's look!"

Overhearing Nancy's comments, Mrs. Flockhart spoke before her daughter could. "Those men could still be on our property. They could be lurking behind the summer house."

"Oh, Mother," Junie said, laughing. "They ran off."

"I know you said that. But if Nancy is right about the paint cans, perhaps they returned for them." She paused a moment. "No, I would prefer that you remain here."

The girl detective, however, was not willing to let such a valuable clue slip past her so easily. "Mrs. Flockhart, would you go with us? I'm sure that two men would not want to tackle three women."

Reluctantly the woman agreed. "All right, but let's be quick about it."

Nancy and Junie hurried outdoors with Mrs. Flockhart behind them and headed for the summer house. Not far from it lay the two empty cans.

"These are the Acme brand," Junie said. "Maybe that will be a clue."

"I think it's a good one," Nancy replied.

She and Junie picked up the two cans and the three went back to the house. At Nancy's suggestion, Junie telephoned each store in town where paint was sold. The first one did not carry this brand.

Nancy waited expectantly, but as someone in each shop said he did not sell the Acme brand, she became more and more discouraged. Her beautiful clue was coming to nothing!

When Junie finished telephoning, she turned to Nancy. "What's the next move? I'm determined to find out who threw that paint at us and ruined your picture!"

"I'm just as determined," Nancy told her. "As you know, Junie, I have never trusted Mr. Rocco from the beginning, and I trust him less now that I know he entered this country under an assumed name or sneaked in. I suggest that we go to his place and look around his barns while avoiding him. Maybe we can find some Acme paint cans."

Junie looked at her friend in astonishment. "That's the last thing in the world I thought you would say, but I agree it's a good idea. I'll get the car."

In a short time Junie parked far from the entrance to Rocco's farm and the two girls walked across the fields toward the barns, which were outside the fenced-in area. They entered one building, which was empty. There were many tools hanging up and shelves on which stood cans of various products, including paint. The girls tiptoed forward to examine them.

"Acme paint!" Nancy whispered. "And, Junie, look! Here is one of blue and one of red in exactly the same shades that were thrown at us."

"So two of Mr. Rocco's workers are guilty!" Junie said in a low tone. "Maybe we'd better hurry away and report the incident before we get caught."

The girls were about to walk outside when they heard voices close by. Two men were speaking in Italian, and they seemed to be arguing.

This went on for a few minutes, then suddenly one of them spoke English. The girls did not recognize the voice that cried out in a snarl, "If they won't join, they won't! And don't ask me to pull any rough stuff to make them do it!"

CHAPTER XIV

Important Information

ASTOUNDED at what they had just heard, Nancy and Junie stood stock-still, staring at each other. They had not recognized the voice of either man.

Instead of tiptoeing away at once, the girls waited to hear more conversation by the two unseen men. There was none, however, and their footsteps faded away.

Nancy at once thought of Eezy and Mrs. Potter, the shopkeeper. Were they being coerced to join some association they wanted to have nothing to do with? Nancy signaled Junie, and the girls walked quickly out of the barn and returned to the car.

As they drove away, Nancy told Junie her suspicions and said, "Let's stop at the general store and see what we can find out from Mrs. Potter."

When they arrived, several people were going

in and out of the store, so Nancy suggested that they wait. "I'd rather talk to Mrs. Potter when no one else is around," she told Junie.

Ten minutes later there seemed to be fewer customers, so the two girls walked into the country store. Mrs. Potter greeted them cordially and asked, "What can I do for you?"

Nancy did not hesitate to tell her the whole story. She asked if her guess had been right about what the two men wanted her to do.

The woman suddenly blushed. "How did you ever figure that out? The whole matter was supposed to be kept secret, otherwise we'd be harmed."

The girl detective smiled. "Junie and I heard it from one of Mr. Rocco's men. Please tell us more."

Mrs. Potter heaved a great sigh and then told the girls that their guess was half right. "There's a lot more to it. Those men who I suspect are tools of Mr. Rocco, found out that I knew the scheme was phony, and threatened me if I told anyone."

"What is the scheme?" Nancy asked.

"They are secretly trying to organize farm workers and employees in small businesses to form a vast association. They are going to fight for higher wages and fringe benefits and all sorts of advantages for the workers."

Junie looked amazed. "Does it include my father's workers?"

"I don't know but I think not. What made me suspicious was that the men demanded money in advance. I suspect they have collected a good bit already. This part I couldn't agree to. But I don't mind telling you that at times I'm afraid those men or some of their pals will come in here and injure me."

Nancy and Junie looked at each other, their thoughts on the attack of Flockhart's shepherd Eezy. As two customers walked into the shop at this moment, the girls quickly purchased some sugarless chewing gum and said good-by to Mrs. Potter.

"Let me hear from you if you find out anything," she called, as they started for the door.

"We will!" Junie replied. After she and Nancy had climbed into the car, she added, "Next stop Eezy's cabin."

As usual they found the elderly shepherd seated in front of his little cabin. He was not playing his Irish harp, but gazing intently over the large flock of sheep he was tending. Near him was the little lamb Nancy liked so much.

Eezy saw the girls trudging up the hillside and waved to them. He spoke to the lamb and apparently it understood what he had said. The animal loped down the slope to meet the girls. They stopped to pet and hug it, then the lamb trotted alongside as they went up the rest of the way to speak to Eezy.

"Cheerio, you get cuter every day," Nancy told the lamb.

When they reached the top of the hillside, Eezy had a treat for them. He had brought out some crackers and glasses of iced lemonade. His visitors thanked him and declared it would taste good after their long hike. As soon as Nancy had finished hers, she got to the subject she had come to quiz him about.

The shepherd listened intently, then suddenly slapped his thigh. "It beats me how you found out, but every word you say is true. I don't go along with the proposition and I don't think anybody else should. I too suspect those men are working for Rocco. I don't trust him and I don't like the idea of collecting money in advance—bah!"

Nancy asked him if he had any idea how far the proposition had succeeded. Eezy said he did not know, but he thought many people had paid and signed up to join his organization.

"But nobody's supposed to talk about it, and I guess that's why no news gets around. The thing that bothers me most is that I think those men may be making progress with some of Mr. Flockhart's workers. He pays us all well, and we're happy at what we're doing. Why should somebody come in here and upset things?

"Besides," he went on, "you know it says in the Good Book, *'Keep thee far from a false matter: for I will not justify the wicked.'* " *

Junie was alarmed by Eezy's theory that many of Mr. Flockhart's workers had been approached and had already secretly joined the organization, giving them an advance payment. She suggested that the girls return at once to the house to talk with her father. The girl detective agreed and the two hurried down the hillside.

Junie's father had just come in. Together the girls told him the startling news.

The man's face became grave. "We can't let this go on!" he declared. "But I must admit that at the moment I don't know exactly how to cope with the situation. I wish I had more data on the subject. Then I'd know how to approach my men."

Nancy had been thinking hard. Now she said to him, "I have a suggestion, Mr. Flockhart. You know my friends are coming here soon for a visit. No one in this neighborhood knows them. How would it be if Ned, Burt, and Dave act as undercover men and find out what they can for you?"

Mr. Flockhart smiled. "That sounds like an excellent idea," he agreed. "I will welcome your friends and ask them to do this detective work, but on one condition."

"What is that?" Nancy asked.

* Exodus 23:7

The big man looked intently at her and said, "I will permit it as long as the work is under the direction of Detective Nancy Drew!"

Nancy laughed. "It's a bargain," she said, and he went off.

A few minutes later a car drove up to the house. Dan White jumped out. Junie rushed outside to greet him, but in a few minutes called to Nancy to join them.

"Danny has a surprise for us," Junie said. "Dan, you tell her."

The college student who was majoring in Italian said that since seeing the girls he had delved into a study of the dialects used in various parts of Italy. "I particularly worked on those spoken by many peasants over forty-five years old, living in different areas of the country. I finally found one that I think Mr. Rocco's workers use. I thought maybe we could run over there and I'll talk to some of the men."

Nancy was thrilled with the idea, so the three set off in Dan's car.

"Let's go to see Tony first," Nancy suggested. "I'd like to know how he's making out with his uncle."

Dan parked the car. He and the girls walked across the fields to the spot where Tony had been hoeing and drawing pictures. He was not there. They looked all over, but did not see him.

"I wonder where he is," Dan said.

"His uncle must have moved him to another field," Junie suggested.

Dan said he could see one of the workmen in the distance and suggested that they walk over so he could talk to him. It was a long trek but finally they reached the man. This time Dan did not say good day in his college Italian, but instead spoke in the dialect he assumed the farmhand might use.

The laborer turned quickly and looked in amazement at the young man. Then he began to speak in a torrent of words. Nancy and Junie wondered how much of it Dan understood. To their delight, he seemed to understand a good bit and answered the man intermittently.

Presently Dan turned to the girls. "What questions do you want me to ask him?"

Nancy said, "Ask him first if he knows where Tony is."

Dan did so and as he listened his brow furrowed. Nancy and Junie wondered what he was being told. Finally Dan turned and translated for the girls.

"This man tells me some very unfortunate news. Tony has run away!"

"Run away!" the girls exclaimed.

Dan said Mr. Rocco had discovered the boy early that morning with a drawing pad and pencil, making sketches instead of hoeing rows of corn.

"His uncle became enraged. He tore the pad to bits and then gave Tony a terrible beating."

"How awful!" Junie said. "I don't blame the poor boy for running away!"

Nancy asked Dan to inquire of the man if he knew where Tony had gone. In response the laborer lifted his arm and pointed toward the Flockhart property.

"We must go after him!" Nancy declared at once. "I'll walk in the direction this man pointed out."

Junie said, "Not alone! After what has happened it would be too dangerous! Dan, how about your going with Nancy? I'll return to your car and drive it home. May I have the keys?"

Dan agreed. He and Nancy set off at a fast pace. They began to run in the direction where Tony was supposed to have gone. Presently the two searchers crossed the boundary between the Rocco farm and Triple Creek.

It seemed to Nancy that there were sheep everywhere but no sign of the boy Tony. Once they stopped to ask a shepherd, but the man declared he had not seen the child.

The couple walked on and presently came to a small ravine with a stream of water at the base. There were no animals in the area, and Nancy assumed that the shepherds tried to keep their flocks away from the dangerous spot.

Suddenly she stopped short. Dan looked at her and said, "Is something the matter?"

"Listen!" she urged. "I heard something."

They both listened and Dan said, "It could be a lamb crying."

Nancy replied, "Yes, it could be. But it sounds more like a child sobbing. Let's head in that direction!"

By listening carefully, the couple decided that it was a human cry coming from near the water at the foot of the ravine. Carefully they descended the steep embankment. In a few minutes they found Tony huddled in a heap and sobbing beside a large rock.

"Tony! Tony!" Nancy exclaimed as she ran toward the boy.

He lifted his tear-stained face and blinked as if he could not believe that Nancy Drew had found his hiding place. He smiled wanly first at her and then at Dan. Then politely he got up and shook hands with each of them.

Dan spoke to him in Italian, repeating what he had heard from the workman on the Rocco farm. Tony replied and Dan translated for Nancy.

"The story is true. Tony says he cannot stand any more of his uncle's cruel treatment. He wants to go to Italy to find his own family."

Nancy suggested that Dan ask him if he knew who they were and if any of them were living. Dan did so and the reply was, "Somebody must be and wouldn't be so mean to me!"

Nancy was touched. What should she do? Take

Tony home with her? Or perhaps she should deliver the boy to State Police headquarters. But they might return him to his uncle!

Then Nancy's eyes glistened as she thought of something. "Dan, I have an idea about what we should do about Tony!"

CHAPTER XV

Secret Notes

"WHAT is your great idea about helping Tony?" Dan asked Nancy.

Excited, she told him of a plan she had suddenly devised. "How would it be if we take him to Eezy for tonight?"

Dan agreed that this would be better than leaving the boy out in the open. "Then what?" he asked.

"We'll get Tony to write a note to his uncle. He can assure Mr. Rocco that he's safe and happy."

Dan urged Nancy to continue. So far he liked her plan.

"I think the note should also say that Tony will return home if his uncle will promise to tell him where the rest of the boy's family is and send him back to Italy."

Dan remarked that this sounded fair enough, but would Rocco keep his word? Then he added, "What about Tony's desire to draw? Isn't it wrong for Mr. Rocco to keep him from doing this?"

Nancy agreed, but said, "I think that solution can come later. We'd better not overdo the request at this time."

Dan felt her decision was a wise one. He added, however, "I can't help but feel that we're letting Mr. Rocco off too easy. I think Tony's note should also warn his uncle that if he doesn't agree to the arrangement, the boy will go at once to the police and report him."

Nancy smiled. "That should throw a scare into the cruel man!"

Dan asked if Nancy intended to take the note to Mr. Rocco herself.

"Oh, no," she replied. "This should be done secretly. He shouldn't know I have anything to do with the case. When I was at the general store, I noticed an old oak tree across the road. It had a deep hollow in the trunk. A note would fit in there perfectly."

Dan wagged his head and grinned. "It's very refreshing and interesting to see a real live detective at work!"

Nancy asked him if he would speak to Tony in Italian and tell him what they had been talking about. Before Dan translated the boy's answers, there was a good bit of conversation between the two. At times Tony would shake his head, at others he would look up at Dan and smile broadly.

Finally Dan was ready to translate. "Tony has agreed to everything," he reported. "He likes the idea of staying with Eezy and knows he will be comfortable and safe there. The only thing he was not sure he wanted to do was threaten his uncle about going to the police. But finally he has agreed to do it. Shall we get started?"

Nancy nodded. The three rose from the ground and walked up the canyon wall. This was difficult. Treacherous, loose stones skidded under their feet.

Dan kept a tight grip on Nancy's arm so that she would not fall. He tried to take Tony's arm with his other hand, but the boy scooted up the precipice with the agility and speed of a mountain goat.

They finally reached the top and walked quickly across the fields to Eezy's cabin. The elderly shepherd was standing up, shading his eyes with one hand, and looking all around. The young people wondered if some of his sheep might have strayed away.

As they drew closer, Eezy's eyes grew large. When they were still a hundred yards away, he shouted at them, "Well, howdy! Howdy! And who is this boy with you?"

Nancy shouted back, "Don't you recognize him? Look closely."

The shepherd shook his head. As Nancy walked closer, she introduced Tony Rocco, then Dan White.

The shepherd laughed. "Oh, Dan and I are old friends. Miss Junie often brings him up here to see me." Then, looking straight at Nancy, he added, "I'll bet you have something interesting to tell me. What is it?"

The girl detective asked him, "How would you like a temporary guest?" The elderly man looked puzzled. Then Nancy explained the plan she and Dan had worked out.

When she told Eezy how Mr. Rocco beat the child, the herdsman scowled. "Fits right in with what I've heard all along about that man. You know I don't like him. I wouldn't trust him a quarter of an acre away."

All this time Tony had stood by, silent and motionless. Now he asked Dan a question in Italian.

Instead of replying, Dan asked Eezy what his answer was. "Why of course I'll take this boy in. I don't get much company up here and it will be fun for me." He asked, "Doesn't Tony speak English?"

"No," Dan replied.

Eezy snapped his fingers. "Then I'm going to start right in teaching him some. Any boy who lives in these United States should speak our language!"

Eezy produced pencil and paper, and Dan helped Tony compose a note to his uncle.

While he was doing this Eezy talked to Nancy. "So the boy was born in Italy and has been here ten years, but has never been allowed to speak anything but Italian."

The shepherd looked off into the clouds, then said, "You know, Nancy, it says in the Good Book, *'It is an ancient nation, whose language thou knowest not, neither understandeth what they say.'* " *

Nancy made no comment but she agreed entirely. It would be interesting to see how fast Eezy could teach Tony some English. "He seems very bright and I'm sure he'll catch on quickly," the girl detective thought.

She reminded Eezy that Tony apparently had great talent as an artist. "While he's here, why don't you give him some paper and pencils and let him sketch? I'm sure that will make the boy very happy."

"I'll start as soon as you folks leave," the shepherd promised.

* Jeremiah 5:15

By this time Tony had finished the note. Dan folded it and put the message into his pocket. As he and Nancy started off, she called back, "We'll return tomorrow." Dan repeated the message in Italian and Tony smiled.

When the two hikers reached the Flockhart farmhouse, they found Junie waiting there with Dan's car. "Tell me what happened!" she urged.

Nancy and Dan told her the whole story. Then they went on to say that they had not discussed Mr. Rocco's possible underhanded deals with Eezy because of Tony's presence.

"When are you going to get in touch with Mr. Rocco?" she asked Dan.

"Right now. I hope he will be at home."

Someone else answered Dan's call. He asked for Mr. Rocco in Italian and wondered what the man on the other end of the line was thinking. "I'm sure he's puzzled," Dan decided, smiling at the situation.

This was confirmed when Mr. Rocco answered. He inquired who the speaker was and where he was from.

Dan did not reply. Instead he said, "Go to the big oak tree opposite the general store for a note to you from Tony." He hung up.

When Dan returned to the girls, Junie asked him, "How soon do you think we should go look for an answer?"

"Not until tomorrow morning," he said. "What do you think, Nancy?"

The girl detective nodded. "For one thing there might be trouble when someone picks up the answer to Tony's message. If so, it would be much better to have it happen in the daylight."

Dan stayed at the Flockharts' overnight. He and the girls were up early to drive to town for a possible answer to Tony's note. They had decided to use his car and to park it some distance from the oak tree, yet close enough so those remaining inside could have a clear view of what was happening.

When they reached the spot, Dan got out and walked quickly up the road to the tree. The girls, who were watching carefully for any attack on him, merely saw him take an envelope from the hollow in the tree, wrinkle his forehead, and then start back to the car.

He jumped in, then said, "What do you make of this?"

The envelope he had picked up had printed words on it, which said, "To the kidnappers of Tony Rocco."

"Kidnappers!" Junie cried out. "We're not kidnappers! We're only trying to help the mistreated boy!"

Nancy did not comment, but was thinking hard. "This is a new angle. If Mr. Rocco has some spies around, they may track us right to Triple

Creek Farm and demand the return of the boy or go to the police and charge the Flockharts and Dan and me with kidnapping!"

This was a twist Nancy had not counted on. By this time Junie had torn open the envelope and removed a slip of paper inside. Again it was addressed to Tony's kidnappers, and read:

> If you are looking for a ransom, forget it. I have nothing to fear from the police, but you certainly have.
>
> Sal Rocco.

While Junie read the note aloud, Nancy looked in all directions to see if she could find any spies. Her eyes became riveted on some heavy bushes a distance in back of the oak tree. Was she mistaken, or did she detect some movement behind it? As she continued to stare, she was positive that two men stood there, peering through the bushes and up the road toward the car.

"Mr. Rocco did have spies!" she decided.

Nancy relayed her thoughts to the others and suggested that Dan take a circuitous route to Triple Creek Farm to throw off pursuit by their enemies. Junie directed Dan to drive down one road and up another and finally all the way through a farm, which had a long lane that exited onto another main road. From here they went home.

As the trio walked into the house, the phone

rang. Junie answered it and called Nancy. "It's for you," she said.

To the young sleuth's delight Ned Nickerson was calling. After a cheery greeting, he said, "If the invitation is still good, Burt, Dave, and I will come up very soon with Bess and George. I hope you have some detective work for us to do."

"Indeed I have," Nancy replied. "A big important job is waiting for you!"

CHAPTER XVI

Reinforcements

ALL that day there was a flurry of excitement in the Flockhart farmhouse. Rooms were prepared for the guests and the refrigerators were filled from the well-stocked cold-storage rooms.

The task was almost completed when the telephone rang. Nancy was closest to the instrument, so she answered the call. It was from Vincenzo Caspari.

"Is that you, Nancy?" he asked. When she told him it was, he said, "I'm so glad I found you at home. I have some very important and exciting news to tell you!"

"Good! What is it?" Nancy asked eagerly.

The artist said he had been in touch with his grandparents in Rome. They in turn had tracked down Diana Bolardo!

"Marvelous!" Nancy exclaimed.

She was tempted to ask him a lot of questions, but she listened silently as Mr. Caspari gave her the rest of his message.

"The young woman is indeed the person who painted the parchment Mr. Flockhart purchased. Incidentally, I did not tell them it had been stolen. They would have wanted to know all the details and I would not have been able to explain." Nancy thought this was probably wise.

"My grandparents reported that *Signora* Bolardo admitted she had painted the parchment picture, but otherwise had been very secretive. One thing she mentioned will surprise and, I am sure, delight you. Diana Bolardo plans to leave at once for the United States. She'll fly over, so she should arrive soon."

Nancy was amazed and delighted to hear this. "Where will she stay in the United States?"

The girl detective could hear Mr. Caspari chuckle at the other end of the phone. "This will be a really big surprise to you," he replied. "She is coming directly to my home and then going to the Flockhart farmhouse!"

Nancy could hardly believe her ears. She was actually going to see and talk to the woman who had made the parchment picture! Again the thought flashed through her mind that the baby in *Signora* Bolardo's picture might be Tony!

Since Vincenzo Caspari had no more to report,

she thanked him for doing this valuable bit of sleuthing, then they said good-by. She rushed off to inform Mrs. Flockhart and Junie of the latest development.

Both of them looked at her unbelievingly. Then a sudden thought occurred to Mrs. Flockhart. She threw up her hands. "One more guest!" she exclaimed. "And she'll want her own room, I'm sure! This house is large but does not have rubber sides! It's going to take some figuring to decide where to put so many people!"

At this moment Mr. Flockhart walked in. He was told the latest news. First Nancy revealed that Bess and George were coming with Ned, Burt, and Dave, then surprised him with the announcement that *Signora* Diana Bolardo was also arriving.

The big man stood in the center of the floor with his feet far apart. He chuckled. "I'd say we're going to have a houseful. How would it be if we put the boys out in a vacant tenant house?"

Junie spoke up. "Oh, Nancy, they are darling houses. I wouldn't mind living in one of them myself."

"That sounds great," Nancy said. "I'm sure the boys will be happy there."

The housecleaning continued for more than an hour, then Nancy and Junie went to one of the tenant houses.

"This place looks spic and span to me," Nancy remarked, walking in.

Junie smiled. "My father is very strict about that. When tenant families move, they are required to leave it clean and tidy."

There was nothing for the girls to do but a little dusting. As soon as this was finished they left. Nancy helped Junie with her farm chores, but all the time she kept thinking about the mystery and the turn it would take when *Signora* Bolardo arrived. It would be exciting, she was sure.

The following morning Ned, Burt, and Dave drove in with Bess and George. As Nancy introduced them to the Flockharts and Dan, she realized how proud she was of her friends.

Ned was tall and good-looking. Burt and Dave were a little shorter. All of them were athletic. Bess and George were cousins but quite different from each other. Bess was a slightly plump blond with dimples. George wore her hair short and was a brunette. She liked plain clothes, whereas Bess tended to admire frills.

"What a wonderful place this is!" Bess exclaimed enthusiastically. "Land, land, as far as you can see."

Dave said, "How would you like to mow six hundred acres of it?"

Junie replied, "We let the sheep do it."

Ned asked, "With a tractor?"

"Sure," said Junie, her eyes twinkling, "We train all our sheep to ride mowers, rake and bail hay, and store it—!"

"Enough!" cried Ned.

After a hearty second breakfast, Dan took the boys to their own house. They changed into farm clothes, then joined the girls, who also were in shirts and jeans.

The boys were eager to be off on their mission. Mr. Flockhart had explained the situation to them and asked that they try to have a full report for him at least by the following evening. Dan joined them and the four drove off, with the girls wishing them luck.

Junie asked Bess and George, "How would you like to have a tour of my father's barns and his factory?"

"Great!" they answered.

Everything went well and the visitors were extremely interested in the work until they came to the slaughterhouse. Then Bess rebelled. She covered her ears with her hands and said, "I can't stand that bleating! Oh those poor things! Why, oh why do they have to be killed?"

Junie, used to this since childhood, smiled. She replied, "They're killed so you and others will have lamb to eat, Bess. Don't you like it?"

Bess said, "Oh, yes, I love it. But don't ask me to watch the slaughter in this barn."

She walked off and returned to the barn where

the baby lambs were. Meanwhile the other three girls went into the slaughterhouse, but after watching the operation a few minutes came out and joined Bess.

"Let's go to the place where your father sells articles made from sheepskins," Bess suggested to Junie.

Nancy said, "I must warn you, Bess. You're going to lose your heart to a lot of things you see in this shop. Watch your pocketbook!"

George was just as intrigued by the sheepskin articles as Bess was. The cousins bought gloves for their parents and treated themselves to after-ski booties.

The tour continued for some time, then the girls drove up the hillside to see Eezy. Though the shepherd was in front of his cabin, Tony was nowhere to be seen. Nancy asked the sheepherder where he was.

After being introduced to Bess and George, Eezy said, "In his schoolroom."

Nancy looked puzzled. "Where is that?"

Eezy took his visitors to a well camouflaged bower beyond the rear of his cabin. They walked inside. Tony was seated on the ground, writing English words.

The boy jumped up and when he was introduced made a low bow to the newcomers. To the amazement of Nancy and Junie he said in perfect

English, "Good morning. I am very glad to see you."

"How wonderful!" Nancy said. "You learn very fast."

Tony was pleased. "Mr. Eezy good teacher," he told the girls.

Bess whispered to George, "Isn't he darling?"

Shyly Tony opened his notebook and showed the girls a sketch of Eezy, which he had made. Nancy and Junie exclaimed in amazement. "It's a marvelous likeness!" Junie remarked, smiling at Tony. "You have a lot of talent."

At this moment Rover came bounding up. He stood still, looking at the group and barking furiously.

"This means," said Junie, "that there is a disturbance somewhere among the sheep. Perhaps some strangers are arriving."

Tony looked frightened. Quickly he gathered up his books and papers and disappeared behind a screen of trees, bushes, and vines.

By this time Eezy had started to follow Rover among the sheep. George puckered her mouth and quipped, "He ought to be called Uneasy!"

Nancy and Junie had already started running after the shepherd, so Bess and George followed. Soon they could see two men trudging up the hill. Their clothes indicated they were law officers. Both wore badges.

When Eezy and his group met the two men, the shepherd asked, "What do you want?"

Without answering him, one of the men asked, "Which of you girls is Nancy Drew?"

When the young sleuth answered, "I am," the same officer said, "Then you are accused of kidnapping Tony Rocco!"

CHAPTER XVII

A Denial and a Chase

THE accusation against Nancy astounded everyone. George, incensed, cried out, "Nancy Drew is not a kidnapper! That's crazy! You'd better leave!"

Nancy, herself, having recovered from the shock, said, "Where are you men from? Show me your credentials."

The spokesman for the two said, "We're from the County Welfare Association and we have the power to make a charge against you and have you arrested!"

All this time Rover was growling at the men. He made a sudden jump toward one of them. The officer kicked him viciously, lifting the dog into the air. Rover came down with a thud and whimpered, but a moment later he was back, ready to attack.

Eezy, who had grabbed his shepherd's crook

when they left the cabin, brandished it in the air. Then he said, "Nancy Drew is not a kidnapper, and I think you two had better get out of here quick before my dog Rover chews you up!"

The man who had not spoken now urged his companion to leave, but the other one stood his ground. "We're taking the guilty girl along with us!" he shouted.

Nancy spoke up. "I am not a kidnapper and I am not going with you!" she declared.

"Oh yes you are!" one of the men snarled and grabbed Nancy's arm. "You're coming with us whether you want to or not!"

His strong fingers dug into Nancy's skin as she tried to wrench herself away. "Let go of me!" she cried, as the man's partner took her other arm.

"Stop it! Stop it!" George shouted at the pair, pulling hard on the second man's wrist.

He released his hold briefly and swung his fist at the girl, who ducked. As she dodged his attack, she got a closer view of his badge.

"C'mon," he said to his companion, "let's get out of here before I really lose my temper."

"Just a minute!" George cried. "I think your badge is phony!"

"Aw, now who's crazy!" her attacker exclaimed.

His partner quickly loosened his grip on Nancy, allowing her to retreat toward Eezy. The other girls stepped forward to look at the badges.

"They certainly look like play badges and not

real ones," Junie remarked, scrutinizing them closely.

The men glanced nervously at each other and tried to sidestep her. "I've got better things to do than play games with a bunch of teenagers!" one man snapped.

Rover was still growling and trying to get out of Eezy's grasp to attack the two strangers. Eezy straightened himself to his full height, brandished his shepherd's crook and bellowed, "Get out of here! And don't ever show your faces here again!"

The intruders, apparently bewildered at this point, suddenly turned and ran down the hillside. Rover tried to get loose from his master and follow them, but Eezy kept a tight hold on his collar.

Suddenly one of the men turned and cried out, "Nancy Drew, don't think you're free! We'll get you yet!"

Nancy was glad to see the men go, but would have liked to find out more about them. She felt sure they were working for Mr. Rocco.

"Let's follow those men!" she urged the others. "Eezy, please let us take Rover. I promise I won't let him hurt them. But I'd like to see where they go."

The shepherd agreed and said he would go back to the cabin. The chase started and the girls managed to get within shouting distance of the men.

Suddenly one of them turned around. He

cupped his hands to his lips and shouted, "You give us back Tony and we'll drop the charge!"

Nancy did not answer. With another thought in mind, she shouted back, "You tell me where the stolen parchment is hidden, and maybe we can manage some kind of a deal!"

There was no answer, although the two men looked at each other as if wondering what to say. They kept quiet, however, and soon reached the foot of the hillside. At the road a car with a driver was waiting for them. The motor was running, and as soon as the men jumped into the vehicle, it took off in a hurry.

Nancy memorized the letters and numbers of the license plate. "It's an out-of-state car! This complicates matters," she thought. "If those men were from some local welfare association, I'm sure they wouldn't be driving an out-of-state car." Then she argued with herself, "But maybe they did it on purpose to avoid identification."

Nancy, Junie, and George had reached the road and stood looking after the fleeing car. Bess had followed at a slower pace. She had seen something glistening on the ground and stooped to pick it up. When she reached the girls, she showed them the shiny object.

"It's one of the phony badges!" Junie cried out. "What a clue!"

Nancy examined it and remarked that there was no identification on it. "I think we should take

One man shouted, "Nancy Drew, we'll get you yet!"

the badge to the police and tell them what happened here.

"Besides," she added, as they started to climb the hillside with Rover, "I noticed that the man who did the talking had a lot of fresh-looking scars on his hand." She paused. "Here's another one of my wild hunches: Do you suppose he could have handled the parchment picture with the broken glass in it? He may be a friend of Sid Zikes."

Junie declared it was worth investigating. When they reached the top of the hill, Nancy showed the badge to Eezy.

He became angry and said, "Those men are nothin' but a couple o' crooks! I've been thinkin' about what they said. I never heard o' any welfare committee around here. They weren't talkin' sense."

Nancy said, "At least we know they're a couple of fakers. My guess is that these are real badges and the men stole them."

At this point Bess heaved a sigh. "Do you realize that George and I have been here less than twenty-four hours, and already we're in the midst of one of Nancy Drew's mysteries? And what a mix-up! We were supposed to help figure out some paintings on a parchment. Instead we are learning the secret of a runaway boy; waiting for the woman who painted the parchment to come from Italy, and looking on as Nancy is accused of being a kidnapper!"

The other girls laughed and George said there was a lot of truth in what Bess had said.

Nancy added, "And now more excitement. I'm going to introduce you to a real thief! Our next stop will be the jail to interview one Sid Zikes!"

CHAPTER XVIII

The First Confession

ALTHOUGH George was intrigued by the idea of meeting a real thief face to face, Bess demurred. "There's no telling what he might do to us," she said. "Besides, he's probably a horrible person with a long record and I don't even want to meet him."

George looked disgusted. "Don't be such a sissy, Bess. The man can't possibly hurt you if he's in jail."

Bess said no more, but when they reached headquarters and were introduced to Officer Browning, she at once changed the subject. Handing him the badge, she asked if it was real or a fake. The officer examined it carefully and even got a magnifying glass.

"This was a police badge," he said, "until someone got hold of it and obliterated all the identification. Where did you find it?"

Nancy told him she had been threatened with "arrest" for kidnapping by two apparently phony county agents. The officer looked grave.

Bess asked, "Why would they tamper with the badges if they were pretending to have authority to take Nancy away?"

Officer Browning said he thought the men were trying to fool the girls, not the police. "But fortunately it didn't work."

George asked, "Then we can assume this badge and the other one were stolen from some policemen?"

"It's a good guess," the officer said. "Suppose you leave the badge here. We'll give it an acid bath and see if we can determine anything about the owner or the phony who was wearing it."

Nancy now asked permission to talk with Sid Zikes. Browning said he had been transferred to the county jail until the date of his trial.

"But I'll be glad to give you a letter to the warden there, and he'll let you in." He looked at the four girls. "Only two visitors are allowed at a time," he remarked.

"You can count me out," Bess said quickly, and George added politely, "And I'll be glad to stay away too," although she was disappointed.

As soon as the note was ready, the four girls rode off. On the way to the county jail, the group became quiet, each girl thinking about some angle of the mystery. Bess's mind was still on the badge,

George was intrigued by Eezy and his influence over the intruders, while Junie kept thinking of young Tony. "How wonderful it would be," she told herself, "if Mrs. Bolardo should turn out to be his mother! But I mustn't get my hopes up too high."

Nancy was alarmed by Mr. Rocco's power and his underhanded method of using other people to extract money from farm workers and swearing them to secrecy.

"He's a sly, untrustworthy person!" she decided. "The sooner we can prove something against him and have him arrested, the better it will be for the whole community."

In a little while the girls reached the county jail and went inside. Almost at once Bess said the atmosphere was too depressing and she would wait outside in the car. She got up and George followed.

"Don't run off with the car and leave us here," Nancy teased.

"It's only a ten-mile walk back," George retorted.

When Nancy and Junie were admitted to Sid Zikes' cell, he looked at them but said nothing. They tried to talk to him but he acted very childish. The young man pouted and declared he had done nothing wrong. "I wouldn't be here if it hadn't been for you, Nancy Drew!" he told her bitterly.

The young detective had decided to talk to the prisoner in a completely different way than she had before. In a gentle voice she said, "Sid, I want to tell you that in case you don't know it, there's a big fraud going on in this area. It won't be long before the whole thing will be known.

"It would be best for you to admit any connection you have with it and act right now rather than wait. We already know of some thefts you have committed. That's bad enough, but to be involved in a really big scheme to defraud is something else again."

Sid looked at the two girls as if he were going to cry. A moment later he began to shake violently. He grabbed a blanket from his cot and wound it around his body.

Finally he said, "I'm not ill. I'm not really cold. I'm shaking from fear. If you'll promise not to tell anyone something I know, which might be part of the fraud you were talking about, I'll tell you a secret."

Nancy and Junie said nothing and apparently Sid Zikes interpreted this as an assent to his request. He went on, "Mr. Rocco has several men working for him—I don't know their names. Two of them came to me and said they wanted the parchment picture that hung over the fireplace in Mr. Flockhart's living room.

"At first I said I wasn't a thief and wouldn't go for any burglarizing. They just laughed and told me they already knew my record. If I didn't do this for them, they would harm me. I guess I'm chicken, but I don't like to be hurt."

Sid went on to say that he had finally agreed to the arrangement. He was to get the picture and take it to the two men at a designated place on the edge of the Rocco farm. He had done this and been paid well for his part in the scheme.

Nancy asked, "Did you deliver it before or after you ordered the new glass?"

"After. I couldn't deliver the picture with the glass broken."

Junie asked him, "Have you any idea where the parchment is now?"

Sid shook his head. "It means nothing to me. The whole point in taking it was that Mr. Flockhart didn't need the picture, but somebody else did. I can't see what's wrong about that."

It flashed through Nancy's mind that here was a person who firmly believed robbing the rich and giving to the poor was perfectly all right. Laws, conscience, and possible harm to an innocent party meant nothing to him!

Nancy looked Sid straight in the eye. He lowered his head but she asked him please to lift it and look at her. She said, "Did it ever occur to you that there's always somebody poorer than yourself?"

The prisoner said no. Nancy went on, "What you have just told me proves that you think it is all right to take something from a person who has a little more than you have yourself." She stared at his right hand. "I see you have on a very good-looking ring."

"The police let me keep it. It's special."

"How would you feel if some really poor boy were to steal it from you?" Nancy asked him.

Sid sat up on the couch. "I'd feel awful. My girl friend gave this to me."

Suddenly the young man looked at Nancy with a totally different expression on his long, lean face. "Hey, I see what you mean. You know, Miss Drew, you've given me an idea. I think maybe I'll go straight from now on."

Nancy and Junie could have leaped for joy. There was something in the tone of Sid's voice that made them think he really meant this. Both of them walked over and shook hands with him and said how glad they were that he had come to this decision.

The prisoner actually smiled. "Hey, thanks an awful lot," he said. "Maybe staying in jail for a short time won't be so bad after all."

At this moment the jailer came and told the girls their visiting time was up. He let them out of the cell. The two waved to Sid, then walked off.

As soon as they reached the street, Junie congratulated Nancy. "It was absolutely marvelous the way you handled Sid."

The girl detective smiled. "Making a prisoner

turn over a new leaf is something I've never done before," she admitted. "I feel good about it myself."

When they reached the car and jumped in, Junie immediately told Bess and George what Nancy had accomplished.

"That's super!" Bess remarked.

"A grand job, Nancy," George commented.

Just before dinnertime at Triple Creek Farm the four boys arrived. They looked weary but were exuberant over the day's achievements.

Ned said, "Mr. Flockhart gave us until tomorrow evening to do our job, but we accomplished so much today, I'm sure it won't be necessary to take tomorrow too."

From a pocket he pulled out a sheet of paper. "Here is a list of people who secretly gave Mr. Rocco money to start his agricultural society. So far we've been told of cash payments for Rocco of fifty to three hundred dollars. We even saw some receipts. When we examined them though, we realized the farmers and a few employees in small businesses never could prove anything from them."

Dan added, "Across the top of the sheet was printed Brotherhood of Agriculturists. It listed the amounts correctly, but the signature at the bottom was a scrawl that nobody could decipher." Nancy wanted to know if the signature was supposed to be Mr. Rocco's.

"The victims all thought it was that of his top man," Ned replied.

Burt spoke up. "This man Rocco is quite an organizer, I'd say. When we totaled up the amount, it proved to be thousands of dollars."

Dave remarked, "If Mr. Flockhart wants us to go ahead, we still have a long list of people to see."

Nancy thought their work was astounding and said so. "But how did you get the people to talk?"

All the boys grinned and Ned said, "Oh, it was easy." He turned to his fellow workers and said, "Shall we tell our secret?"

CHAPTER XIX

A Strange Reunion

As Ned and the other boys delayed telling the story of obtaining statements from people who had given Sal Rocco's henchmen money, Nancy urged them to begin.

"All right," Ned said. "The boys and I pretended without saying so that we are already members of the association." He grinned. "We must be pretty convincing because nobody questioned us."

Burt took up the story. "We said we were becoming very suspicious of Mr. Rocco because we had heard nothing from him. We learned that nobody else had, either."

"In fact," Dave put in, "by the time we had talked to each one for a while, we felt convinced that most of the people were ready to protest. Each person was reluctant to be the one to organize a march on Rocco's men."

Dan said that a few people had telephoned the

Rocco home and had tried to get some information. "The owner either was not there or refused to come to the phone."

Nancy asked, "So they didn't learn anything?"

Ned shook his head. "The farmers who did talk to one of Rocco's men were assured that everything was fine and that they would hear about an organization meeting soon."

Dan added, "Each of those callers got a lecture on helping unfortunate people, which was the same one they had received when being asked to join the association."

Burt remarked, "It's quite a lingo that Rocco has worked up. At first I was inclined to believe it myself!"

George asked, "What I'd like to know is, where is Mr. Rocco keeping all the money he had his men collect?"

"Good question," Dan replied. "I know the president of the local bank. How about my phoning him to see if Mr. Rocco made a lot of deposits there?"

The others thought this was a good idea, so Dan called. The answer, however, was disappointing. Mr. Rocco kept an account there from which he drew checks to pay bills and get small amounts of cash, but he had never deposited large amounts. Most of the income was from products sold from his farm.

Junie heaved a sigh. "Another dead-end clue!"

The others laughed, then Bess asked Nancy, "Have you any hunches about what Mr. Rocco might have done with the money?"

"I've been thinking about it," the young sleuth replied. "It's possible that he has hidden the cash right on his own farm."

"On his own farm?" Bess repeated.

"Sure, there are a million places he could hide his money—in an old suitcase, atop the loft in a barn—"

"He could've planted it in the cornfield!" the plump girl quipped.

"Or in the bottom of a well!" her cousin added.

"Stop teasing Nancy," Ned said, circling his arm around her shoulder. "She's trying to solve a mystery and—"

Nancy smiled warmly at her friend. "I can always count on you for help, though," she said, causing the boy's face to redden.

"Maybe we ought to leave the lovebirds alone, Bess, to figure out this case," George put in.

"Now, now," Nancy replied. "I need everybody's ideas."

Further conversation was interrupted by the ring of the telephone. Junie went to answer it. During her absence the others began asking one another questions on angles of the mystery.

"What I can't understand," said Bess, "is why Mr. Rocco is so mean and cruel to his young nephew."

They all decided that this was an important part of the mystery and they hoped it would soon be cleared up.

Dan said, "I'm sure the authorities will take this boy away and put him in a school or a home where he will be given kindness."

At this moment Junie rushed back into the room. "Guess what?" she said. "Mrs. Bolardo has arrived in this country. Right now she is at Mr. Caspari's house. She wants to come over here at once so she can see her son."

"Her son!" the others in the room cried out.

Junie said the artist had told her that the full story had to wait until Mrs. Bolardo arrived at the Flockhart farm. "He's going to bring her right over, but it's a fairly long drive."

The girl's announcement had come like a real bombshell to the listeners. So Tony's real name was Tony Bolardo! While waiting for Mr. Caspari to drive in, the group of young people tried to work, but found themselves gathering to discuss the mystery.

Bess remarked, "It's getting more exciting by the minute!"

Finally Mr. Caspari arrived with the woman artist from Italy. She proved to be beautiful and charming. Both Mr. and Mrs. Flockhart had come to meet her, and she returned their welcome in perfect English. After the pleasantries were over, her expression changed.

"My son! Where is he? I want to see him at once! He was stolen from me!" she cried out.

Mrs. Flockhart sat down on the sofa beside her and took the woman's hand in hers. "Please tell us the whole story from beginning to end," she requested.

If she had hoped to calm Mrs. Bolardo, she failed. With each sentence the artist uttered, she became more emotional. "What does my son Tony look like?" she asked.

Nancy told her that he was a handsome child. "He looks like you and he shows great promise as an artist."

"Oh, I am so glad, I am so glad!" Mrs. Bolardo said. "But tell me where he is. I want to see him!"

Junie told her that they had Tony hidden away and would go to see him in a little while.

"We took him away from his uncle because the man was mean and cruel to him."

"That dreadful man!" Mrs. Bolardo exclaimed. "I will tell you the whole story. My husband and I were very happily married and excited beyond words when little Tony was born. My husband had some business to take care of, so he went off on a steamer. Unfortunately it was in an accident with a sailing vessel, and he was killed."

"That's terrible!" Bess murmured.

Mrs. Bolardo went on to say that her husband's brother Salvatore was the executor of her husband's estate.

"Sal wanted me to marry him but I refused. In revenge Sal took all the money that was left to me, stole my precious baby, and disappeared. I have searched and searched for them, but until now, never had a lead."

Tears began to trickle down Bess's cheeks. She wiped her eyes with a handkerchief and remarked, "For ten years you never heard about them?"

Mrs. Bolardo shook her head.

George mentioned that Tony's name was not really Tony Rocco, but Tony Bolardo. His mother said that actually his full name was Antonio Rocco Bolardo. The name Rocco was his paternal grandmother's before she married.

The woman artist continued, "Right after my husband's death I painted four pictures on parchment to tell the story. Little Tony's abductor also took that."

"So you are the woman in one painting!" Junie exclaimed, and Mrs. Bolardo nodded.

Nancy said she was sorry she could not show the parchment to the woman because it had been stolen. "I made some rough sketches in imitation of it," she said. "But the real clues to finding you were the initials on the back of your picture."

Mrs. Bolardo suddenly stood up. "Please take me to my boy!" she pleaded. "Where is he?"

Everyone felt convinced that the woman was not an impostor. It was decided that she and Nancy would go alone to Eezy's cabin.

Mr. Flockhart added, "I think it best if we form ourselves into a group of guards. We can station ourselves around the hillside among the sheep, so that if any of Mr. Rocco's men follow Mrs. Bolar o and Nancy, we can head them off."

Nancy said, "Wouldn't it be a good idea also to inform the police of what has happened and to send men out to keep track of Mr. Rocco?"

The farm owner thought this was a very good suggestion and went at once to phone the police. He talked to Officer Browning, who promised to take care of all the details.

Junie spoke up. "Dad, wouldn't it be a good idea to try getting Mr. Rocco into his own house and to be there when we all come with Tony and his mother?"

"I'll mention that to Officer Browning," her father agreed.

Several cars were to be used in the operation. Nancy and Mrs. Bolardo rode in one, in the center of the line. Each car parked at a different place, and the group walked up the hillside in twos and threes.

"This is lovely country," Mrs. Bolardo remarked to Nancy when they got out. "I guess it has been a good healthy place to bring up Tony. But it is dreadful that he has never been to a school or made any friends."

Most of the sheep were lying down, and the two climbers walking among them did not seem to disturb the animals. It was so quiet that Nancy mentioned it to her companion.

"I don't see the shepherd either," Nancy said as she gazed around, realizing the man was not at his usual station in front of the cabin. They walked up and called out his name, but there was no answer.

Nancy peered inside the cabin. No one was there! The girl thought this was very strange, and suddenly began to worry that something had happened to the elderly man. And what about Tony?

Without showing the agitation she felt, the girl detective told Mrs. Bolardo that Tony worked and studied in a well-hidden bower behind the cabin. Carefully they proceeded, parting branches of trees and shrubbery as they went.

Finally they reached the arbor and looked in. Mrs. Bolardo screamed and Nancy caught her breath. Eezy and Tony had been trussed up, and were lying inert on the ground!

"Oh, how dreadful!" Mrs. Bolardo cried out. "My son! My beloved boy! What have they done to you?"

Nancy jumped forward to remove the gags and ropes that bound the two tightly. Before she could reach them, strong arms came around her and yanked the girl backward. Mrs. Bolardo received the same treatment.

"Let me go!" Nancy cried out, struggling to pull free of her captor.

"Be quiet or you'll get something worse!" her unknown assailant hissed into her ear.

Nancy glanced at Mrs. Bolardo. A man was holding one hand tightly over the woman's chest and was stuffing a gag into her mouth!

CHAPTER XX

Found Money

THE men who had captured Nancy and Mrs. Bo-lardo were masked and wore dark coveralls. She could not identify her assailants.

They trussed up Nancy and the Italian woman as they had Eezy and Tony. No doubt they had just finished their work on the shepherd and the boy when they heard voices and spotted the girl and her companion coming up the hillside.

Nancy could hardly wait for the two men to leave. Surely the boys would capture the attackers somewhere among the sheep as they hurried away. Besides, she wanted to try untying some of the knots that bound Eezy's wrists.

There was a moment of panic for the prisoners when one of the captors lifted Tony and swung the boy over his shoulder. He was going to take him away! The other captor whispered something in his ear, however, and the man laid down his victim. "We'll come back for you after dark," he told Tony.

"Evidently they're afraid to go any farther at this time," Nancy thought.

Finally the dark-clothed figures left. At once Nancy wiggled over to Eezy's side. He understood what she wanted to do, and rolled over. It took her several minutes to free his hands. In turn, he untied the knots of the ropes that bound her wrists. After that it did not take long to remove all the gags and untie their ankles.

Mrs. Bolardo had been so frightened she seemed speechless, but Nancy said, "Tony, I have a wonderful surprise for you. This is your mother!"

The boy stared, unbelieving, but Mrs. Bolardo rushed to him and hugged her child. "Tonio! Tonio!" she exclaimed, and then went on, speaking rapidly in Italian.

At first Tony could not believe what he had heard, but as his mother talked and told him about his own kidnapping and his thieving uncle, he believed her story and put his arms around her.

All this time Eezy had stood by, speechless. He swung his head from side to side, and kept mumbling, "I can't believe it!"

Mrs. Bolardo heard him. She let go of Tony and addressed herself to the shepherd. "It is true! And the main part of the credit goes to wonderful Nancy Drew!"

Tony now surprised them all by saying in perfect English, "Thank you. Thank you very much. This is a very happy day for me and my mother."

Nancy asked if she might use Eezy's walkie-talkie. "I'd like to tell the good news to everyone down at Triple Creek."

The little group walked back to the cabin and Nancy called. Mrs. Flockhart answered and was thrilled to hear that mother and son were together after all these years. She was not happy, however, to learn that the four of them had been attacked by men who apparently were in Mr. Rocco's employ.

"I'll notify the police at once about what has happened," she said.

Nancy had just finished the conversation, when she saw Bess, George, Ned, Burt, Dave, Dan, and Junie coming up the hillside. They waved gaily and Ned called out, "We captured your attackers! They've confessed!"

When the group drew close, Ned explained that the young people were hiding at various posts behind the sheep and trees, and saw the two coveralled men racing down the hillside. They were speaking in Italian but Dan could understand them.

"We realized from their conversation what had happened up here, so we ran after them," he said. "Right now they're in the hands of the police."

"That's great!" Nancy exclaimed, then properly introduced those present.

Mrs. Bolardo and Tony stood together, arm in arm, looking delighted at the turn of events. Then a walkie-talkie message came from Mr. Flockhart, advising that everyone except Eezy was to proceed at once to the Rocco home. He did not explain why, but everyone assumed that Rocco had been arrested.

Tony, excited, said in Italian, "I know a short-cut." He bid Eezy good-by and thanked him for his good care and fine meals. Then the boy led the others down a different section of the hillside.

It was not long before the Rocco farmhouse was in sight. Ned, who had been walking with Nancy, had been very quiet, but now he said, "See all those people down there? Burt, Dave, and I got hold of the farmers and others who had joined the association. We suggested they come to Rocco's place."

Now the farmers and other residents of the area were milling around, talking. As Nancy and her companions came closer, she noticed that some of the crowd looked angry and a few were trying to get into the house. Police guarded the door and kept them out. By the time Nancy and her friends reached it, Mr. Flockhart was there and told the guard to admit them.

They found Mr. Rocco seated on his living-room couch, being quizzed by a police officer. He had denied every accusation.

Suddenly he looked up and blinked as he saw

Tony and Diana Bolardo, arm in arm, standing before him.

Without speaking to them, the man jumped from the couch and dashed for the door. He was caught by a policeman and escorted back into the living room.

Finally he managed to say, "Diana! Diana! How did you get here? How did you find me? I meant no harm taking your baby. I felt that you would not be able to take care of him."

"That was because you stole all my money!" the woman cried out. "Salvatore, you are a wicked man. How glad I am that these good people here were able to bring Tony and me together again so you can't do him any more harm!"

Rocco looked defiant. "I did not harm him, and have brought him up right. I hope you will find it in your heart to forgive me for taking Tony."

His sister-in-law made no response. At this moment there was a great shout from outside, and voices calling, "We want Rocco! We want Rocco!"

"I'm not going out there!" the man declared.

"Oh yes you are," one of the police guards said.

He took Rocco by the arm and walked him onto the porch so that he could face his accusers. Rocco still denied any wrongdoing, but they insisted upon his returning their money.

Rocco, livid, shouted, "All right! You can have your money back if you can find it!" He turned and went back into the living room.

Ned whispered to Nancy, "It's my guess that the money is hidden on the premises. How would it be if the other boys and I help these farm workers find it?"

"Good idea," Nancy said, and the great search started.

She went inside, where Rocco was again seated on the couch, with police guards on either side of him. He looked sullen and angry. His black eyes kept darting toward his sister-in-law as if he could not believe she was really there.

Nancy noticed that between glances, the man's eyes kept roving toward a table with a large drawer in it. The girl detective wondered if there might be something in it that he did not want anybody to see.

She called one of the policemen aside and asked him to investigate. As the two walked toward the table, Rocco suddenly got up and tried to escape. He was soon stopped and brought back. The second guard rejoined Nancy, and they opened the long drawer in the table.

Inside lay the stolen parchment picture!

"Oh!" Nancy exclaimed. She turned to Rocco. "You had Sid Zikes steal this picture, hoping the secret it contains wouldn't be found out!"

Rocco shouted, "I never should have sold the picture! I should have destroyed it long ago! I never saw the initials on the back, but when I heard Nancy Drew was working on the case, I decided to steal it!"

At this moment one of the men who lived in the house came into the room. He went over and addressed Rocco.

"You fooled a lot of people, Sal, but you didn't fool me, although I admit your threats frightened me into being your puppet. I haven't forgotten how you cheated me and my family years ago, and I was determined to get even at some time. You knew the secret locked in the parchment picture and I knew it too! But I didn't know where Tony's mother was and whether she was alive or not. When you sold the picture I saw a good chance for somebody else to figure out the secret and bring you to justice.

"After you sold the picture to Mr. Flockhart, I telephoned him that if he could decipher the meaning of the paintings, he would learn a great secret and right an old wrong."

No one in the room was more surprised at this revelation than Nancy Drew. Now all the questions concerning the strange mystery had been solved.

Nancy looked at the informer quizzically. "How much did you have to do with getting money from farmers to join an association?"

"Nothing," he replied. "My name is Hapgood. I have been telling Sal that he ought to get the

association started or give back the money. But he
wouldn't pay any attention to me."

Suddenly Rocco screamed at him, "Hapgood,
get out of here and never let me see you again!
You are a cheat and a double-crosser!"

Hapgood did not move. He turned to the police
guard and said, "I am innocent and I hope to get
some credit for helping to straighten out matters
at this place and restore Tony to his rightful
mother. Most of the field workers, as well as Sal,
sneaked into this country illegally."

One of the policemen said, "That's not for me
to decide. You will be questioned with all the
other men who work here."

Just then there was a great shout from outdoors.
Everyone rushed to the porch except Rocco and
his guards. Ned Nickerson ran up to Nancy.

"All the stolen money and the names of the
people have been discovered!"

"Where?" Nancy asked.

Ned told her that some of it had been found in
an abandoned well, other cash in the hayloft, under the car seat of Rocco's automobile, and the
account book in one of the barns.

Farmers and others involved had appointed
Mrs. Potter their chairman. Now she was busy
giving out the proper amounts of money to each
person who had contributed to the fake association.

Burt and Dave came up and said they had located a cage of mechanical birds, which had attacked Nancy and Junie on their first visit to the Rocco farm.

"We understand from the man who worked the mechanism by remote control that Mr. Rocco believed the lifelike birds would drive off intruders. He would not be blamed, however, because the victims would think the birds were alive."

Finally the crowd outdoors dispersed, happy at the outcome. Mrs. Potter spoke for them all and thanked Nancy for her part in keeping them from losing so much money.

Nancy was thoughtful for a moment as she realized this mystery was solved. Little did she know that she would soon become involved in the exciting *Mystery of Crocodile Island.*

In the meantime, more police arrived. Every worker on the Rocco farm was rounded up and word came that other henchmen of Rocco's were being sought.

After everyone had gone, Mr. Flockhart came into the house and talked with Mrs. Bolardo about her plans.

"Oh, as soon as we can get Antonio's clothes packed and buy him some new ones, we'll set off for Italy."

Mr. Flockhart insisted that they stay at his home until the woman and her son were ready to fly to New York and then to Rome. She accepted the invitation, then looked at her son lovingly.

"Italy is where Tonio belongs," she told the group, "but I promise you all that his English will not be neglected. I plan to send him to a special school where children learn many languages and talented young artists get fine training from the masters."

"That's great," Nancy said. "Tony, I'm counting on you. Someday I hope to see many beautiful paintings by Antonio Rocco Bolardo."

He tried to speak English, but gave up, and finished in Italian. His mother translated, then told Nancy the boy's smiling answer.

"I won't disappoint you, I promise. But in the meantime, please keep up your own interest in art, Nancy. It helped you solve the mystery of the parchment and gave me back my lovely mother!"

Order Form
Own the original 58 action-packed
HARDY BOYS MYSTERY STORIES®

In *hardcover* at your local bookseller OR
simply mail in this handy order coupon and start your collection today!

Please send me the following Hardy Boys titles I've checked below.
All Books Priced @ $5.99

AVOID DELAYS   Please Print Order Form Clearly

☐ 1	Tower Treasure	448-08901-7	☐ 30	Wailing Siren Mystery	448-08930-0
☐ 2	House on the Cliff	448-08902-5	☐ 31	Secret of Wildcat Swamp	448-08931-9
☐ 3	Secret of the Old Mill	448-08903-3	☐ 32	Crisscross Shadow	448-08932-7
☐ 4	Missing Chums	448-08904-1	☐ 33	The Yellow Feather Mystery	448-08933-5
☐ 5	Hunting for Hidden Gold	448-08905-X	☐ 34	The Hooded Hawk Mystery	448-08934-3
☐ 6	Shore Road Mystery	448-08906-8	☐ 35	The Clue in the Embers	448-08935-1
☐ 7	Secret of the Caves	448-08907-6	☐ 36	The Secret of Pirates Hill	448-08936-X
☐ 8	Mystery of Cabin Island	448-08908-4	☐ 37	Ghost at Skeleton Rock	448-08937-8
☐ 9	Great Airport Mystery	448-08909-2	☐ 38	Mystery at Devil's Paw	448-08938-6
☐ 10	What Happened at Midnight	448-08910-6	☐ 39	Mystery of the Chinese Junk	448-08939-4
☐ 11	While the Clock Ticked	448-08911-4	☐ 40	Mystery of the Desert Giant	448-08940-8
☐ 12	Footprints Under the Window	448-08912-2	☐ 41	Clue of the Screeching Owl	448-08941-6
☐ 13	Mark on the Door	448-08913-0	☐ 42	Viking Symbol Mystery	448-08942-4
☐ 14	Hidden Harbor Mystery	448-08914-9	☐ 43	Mystery of the Aztec Warrior	448-08943-2
☐ 15	Sinister Sign Post	448-08915-7	☐ 44	The Haunted Fort	448-08944-0
☐ 16	A Figure in Hiding	448-08916-5	☐ 45	Mystery of the Spiral Bridge	448-08945-9
☐ 17	Secret Warning	448-08917-3	☐ 46	Secret Agent on Flight 101	448-08946-7
☐ 18	Twisted Claw	448-08918-1	☐ 47	Mystery of the Whale Tattoo	448-08947-5
☐ 19	Disappearing Floor	448-08919-X	☐ 48	The Arctic Patrol Mystery	448-08948-3
☐ 20	Mystery of the Flying Express	448-08920-3	☐ 49	The Bombay Boomerang	448-08949-1
☐ 21	The Clue of the Broken Blade	448-08921-1	☐ 50	Danger on Vampire Trail	448-08950-5
☐ 22	The Flickering Torch Mystery	448-08922-X	☐ 51	The Masked Monkey	448-08951-3
☐ 23	Melted Coins	448-08923-8	☐ 52	The Shattered Helmet	448-08952-1
☐ 24	Short-Wave Mystery	448-08924-6	☐ 53	The Clue of the Hissing Serpent	448-08953-X
☐ 25	Secret Panel	448-08925-4	☐ 54	The Mysterious Caravan	448-08954-8
☐ 26	The Phantom Freighter	448-08926-2	☐ 55	The Witchmaster's Key	448-08955-6
☐ 27	Secret of Skull Mountain	448-08927-0	☐ 56	The Jungle Pyramid	448-08956-4
☐ 28	The Sign of the Crooked Arrow	448-08928-9	☐ 57	The Firebird Rocket	448-08957-2
☐ 29	The Secret of the Lost Tunnel	448-08929-7	☐ 58	The Sting of the Scorpion	448-08958-0

Also Available The Hardy Boys Detective Handbook 448-01990-6

**VISIT PUTNAM BERKLEY ONLINE
ON THE INTERNET: http://www.putnam.com/berkley**

Payable in U.S. funds. No cash accepted. Postage & handling: $3.50 for one book. $1.00 for each additional. Maximum postage $8.50. Prices, postage and handling charges may change without notice. Visa, Amex, MasterCard call 1-800-788-6262, ext. 1, or fax 1-201-933-2316.

Or, check above books
and send this order form to:

**The Putnam Publishing Group
P.O. Box 12289, Dept. B
Newark, NJ 07101-5289**

Please allow 4-6 weeks for delivery.
Foreign and Canadian delivery 8-12 weeks

Bill my: ☐ Visa ☐ MasterCard ☐ Amex _____ (expires)

Card#_____
                                                    ($10 minimum)

Daytime Phone # _____

Signature_____

Or enclosed is my: ☐ check ☐ money order
SHIP TO:
Name _____
Address _____
City _____ State _____ Zip _____

BILL TO:
Name _____
Address _____
City _____ State _____ Zip _____

Book Total	$ _____
Applicable Sales Tax (CA, NJ, NY, GST Can.)	$ _____
Postage & Handling	$ _____
Total Amount Due	$ _____

Nancy Drew® and The Hardy Boys® are trademarks
of Simon & Schuster, Inc. and are registered
in the United States Patent and Trademark Office.